TRAIL OF
CRUMBS

TRAIL OF CRUMBS

LISA J. LAWRENCE

ORCA BOOK PUBLISHERS

Library and Archives Canada Cataloguing in Publication

Lawrence, Lisa J., 1975–, author
Trail of crumbs / Lisa J. Lawrence.

Issued in print and electronic formats.
ISBN 978-1-4598-2121-7 (softcover).—ISBN 978-1-4598-2122-4 (PDF).—
ISBN 978-1-4598-2123-1 (EPUB)

I. Title.
PS8623.A9266T73 2019   jc813'.6   c2018-904898-0
c2018-904899-9

Library of Congress Control Number: 2018954142
Simultaneously published in Canada and the United States in 2019

Summary: In this young adult novel, Greta and her twin brother are abandoned by their father and stepmother, and Greta struggles with the confusion and shame she feels after being raped.

Orca Book Publishers is dedicated to preserving the environment and has printed this book on Forest Stewardship Council® certified paper.

Orca Book Publishers gratefully acknowledges the support for its publishing programs provided by the following agencies: the Government of Canada, the Canada Council for the Arts and the Province of British Columbia through the BC Arts Council and the Book Publishing Tax Credit.

Edited by Sarah N. Harvey
Cover illustration by Sofía Bonati
Cover design by Teresa Bubela
Author photo by Michael Lawrence

ORCA BOOK PUBLISHERS
orcabook.com

Printed and bound in Canada.

22 21 20 19 • 4 3 2 1

To Fast Eddie (LMW), for thirty-three years of shenanigans and approximately 1,200 boxes of Kraft Dinner, and to all the Gretas of the world, wherever you are in your journey

ONE

Greta always thought of Patty as a person of gaps—gaps between her teeth and her skinny thighs, gaps in logic. When Patty laughed, it reminded Greta exactly of a barking seal. But she wasn't laughing now. She was lecturing Ash and Greta on how much toilet paper they'd gone through in a week, like they had single-handedly used it all themselves.

"I shouldn't be buying this *all the time*," Patty said, glaring back and forth between them.

"Then stop using it yourself." Ash shrugged, tapping his fingers on the tabletop. "In some parts of the world, they just use their hands."

"Hey!" Patty shouted. "I don't need your lip! Get a job and start pulling your weight."

"Maybe I will," Ash said, pushing past her. "Then I can move out."

"Good idea!" she yelled through the empty doorway.

"Or why don't *you* get a job," Ash said, "so you can move out instead."

During Patty's flurry of cursing, Greta let herself out the front door, climbing the steps of the concrete stairwell cave. Across the street their neighbor vacuumed the interior of his yellow Volvo, both doors hanging open. He straightened and waved to Greta. He was tall and pale with a nest of ginger hair. Slightly buggy eyes and an open face. Greta recognized him from Ash's English class. He watched her as if she might stop and talk. She walked faster, checking over her shoulder to make sure he hadn't followed her.

Greta circled the block a few times, crunching the brittle ice of unshoveled walks. Snow heaped in knee-high dunes on either side. Bleak January afternoon, like the sun never fully rose. Before going back inside, she listened at the bottom of the steps. All quiet.

No one in the living room. Greta tapped on her brother's door—technically the storage room—and opened it when he didn't answer.

He lay on a rumpled single mattress, staring at a bare bulb dangling from a wire. The back wall was covered with wide, rough shelves—the kind you'd put boxes or canned goods on. Ash had piled a few books there, but the shelves sat mostly empty. No windows. She sat on the bed next to him.

"Why did Dad marry her?" she asked, not really expecting an answer.

"So he wouldn't have to think anymore," Ash said.

"What do you mean?"

He propped himself up on an elbow to face her. "If Patty knows everything and decides everything, what does Roger have to worry about?" Ash had started calling their father by his first name a few years back. It drove Patty crazy.

Greta thought about this, how lost their father had been after their mom died. She nodded. It made sense. Patty—dictator of a country too tired to retaliate. "Time for a coup?"

He smiled and shook his head. "Don't think it'll work."

Ash was right. There was no military in this country. Just one despot and a few unarmed civilians.

.....

Their dad called a family meeting when he got home from work. "Patty says there's been some disrespect," he said.

They sat in a circle around the kitchen table, which was practically in the living room. The basement suite squeezed all the furniture into the same space. Roger pinched his eyebrows together and tried to look stern, but Greta noticed his jowls—the loose skin trembling around his jaw as he spoke. His blue eyes watered, and she could see his scalp through his thinning gray-blond hair. He looked old.

Patty nodded smugly. She stopped to give a wheezing cough and resumed nodding. Greta, distracted by the bobbing of Patty's yellowish perm, forgot to answer. Ash glowered at Roger and Patty across the table.

"Yes," Ash said, clearing his throat, "I'd like to lodge a complaint against Patty for interfering with how I wipe myself."

"Ash…" Roger warned.

"You see?" Patty said. "This is exactly what I'm talking about. Thank you, Ash, for illustrating my point. Roger…"

Roger held up his hands in a time-out.

"Let me know when Patty gives you your balls back, Roger," Ash said, pushing away from the table and walking to his storage closet. The door, hanging crooked in its frame, only made a *thunk* when he tried to slam it.

Patty started shouting, and Roger lowered his head into his hands.

"Can I go now? I've got homework," Greta lied. No one was listening anyway.

She got up from the table and went to her room. It wasn't much bigger than Ash's closet, but at least it actually was a bedroom, with a window, a bed off the floor and a dresser. At some point someone had painted the walls a deep burgundy, but all the dents and gashes revealed a sickly yellow underneath. *It's temporary.* She told herself that every time she noticed the basement swallow any sunlight, every time a fungus-shaped frost crept up the inside of the windows, every time she saw Ash staring up at the bare bulb in the storage room. *Temporary.*

They hadn't even discussed who got the bedroom. That was the worst part. Roger and Patty had just dropped her boxes in here during the last move. "I guess I'll take this… room," Ash had said, eyeing the storage space. "I'm sure it's up to code."

Patty gave him a look and said, "Suck it up, Buttercup."

No one came out and said it, but in the country run by Dictator Patty, Ash was a fast-food worker or possibly homeless.

What he got he was expected to accept without complaint. Roger was, at best, a spineless government advisor. Greta was probably a small-business owner, struggling to get by, whining about taxes.

She could still hear them with the door closed. How did Ash do that? Patty got mad at Ash. Roger got mad at Ash, and Ash got Patty mad at Roger and walked away without a scratch.

Greta picked up her phone and ran her thumb over the screen with a crack in one corner, wanting to text someone. Rachel? No. Definitely not. It annoyed her that the impulse still lingered. She and Ash shared the phone, but Ash had basically given it to her. "I don't have anyone to call," he'd said. Greta always saw him alone at school, if she saw him at all. When she invited him to hang out with her, he just shook his head and disappeared. For twins in the same grade, they rarely crossed paths. Ash had a way of doing that—disappearing into shadows, corners, storage closets. She envied that about him.

When Roger and Patty went quiet, Greta eased the door open a crack. She could see their heads still bent together at the table. The last thing Greta wanted was to be called back to finish the toilet-paper conversation. Every time Patty opened her mouth, Greta felt more misery heaped on the pile. It was the last thing she needed. She took a soft step into the hallway, toward the open bathroom door. Then froze.

"...can't just leave..." Roger whispered.

"Not forever. Of course not."

Roger shook his head.

The words *just leave* paralyzed Greta. What did he mean? Coming from her father's mouth, those words didn't make sense—a foreign language.

"How are they ever going to learn responsibility?" Patty asked.

"They're still in school!" Roger's voice rose to near-normal, and Patty shushed him. Greta darted back to her bedroom, flicking off the light but leaving the door open.

"I worked all through high school," Patty said. "I know the value of a dollar."

"It doesn't seem right." He sounded tired.

"Well, this isn't right either—mooching off you, expecting everything on a silver platter. How are we ever going to get into a house while we're dragging all this around?"

Greta almost snorted out loud. Dragging *this* around— two heavy rocks. And the silver platter? After their mom died, when Greta and Ash were eight, it had been a steady downward spiral to this—a damp basement suite with a yellow-permed scarecrow. Greta remembered how Roger, after the funeral, had been home with them, sleeping a lot. After a few months he'd tried going back to driving truck, leaving them with his sister, Aunt Lori, for weeks at a time. Then he'd gotten a DUI and lost that job. He'd sold their house, and they had stayed with Aunt Lori for a while. The following year they had moved two—three?—more times, now a blur of stark walls and industrial carpets. Then to the condo on the north side, and Roger started driving again.

That's when he met Patty, and there was a sense that life was firm again. Greta opened her eyes in the morning and knew where she would sleep that night, and the next. Patty worked in a restaurant and brought them warm pizza every Friday night. They took trips to the park, with ice-cream cones from McDonald's. For their tenth birthdays, Patty bought Ash a remote-controlled car, and Greta a red dress. It was the first new dress she'd gotten in two years.

Roger and Patty got married later that year, and then the fighting started. Patty quit her job at the restaurant "to look after the kids." Only she wasn't usually up when they left for school and wasn't around when they got home. She called family meetings about the chores Greta and Ash didn't get done or didn't do well enough. For seven years Greta had watched the lines grow deeper on her father's face, his hair thin across his scalp. Any suggestion, from anyone, that Patty get a job provoked a tirade about how no one appreciated all her hard work around the house. Greta wasn't sure exactly what Patty did besides opening bills and shouting about them.

They had moved into the basement suite over the summer, after being slapped with a three-hundred-dollar-a-month rent increase at the north-side condo. "Three hundred dollars more, for one bathroom and carpets from the seventies?" Patty had howled. For once Greta hadn't disagreed. Then her dad had found the basement suite on the west end, and he and Patty talked about living cheaply to save up for their own house. They moved just in time for Greta and Ash to start their last year of school at West Edmonton High.

It was either that or an hour-and-a-half bus ride each way to their old school.

"We're moving in our graduating year?" Greta had complained, but only out of duty. One of her best friends had moved to Kelowna in June and hadn't called or texted since, and the other had drifted into a different group. Greta felt exposed—the last bird in the nest.

So this was their silver platter. Greta took a deep breath to stop herself from bursting through the door and throat-punching Patty. Six months from graduation, and Patty had decided they needed to learn responsibility. This from the woman who hadn't worked a day in seven years.

"I've given up a lot to join this family and play mother to those kids," Patty continued, "and they don't appreciate a single thing." Roger started to say something, but she cut him off. "It's time for you to choose, Roger. I won't be made homeless by those two." She pushed back her chair and stomped away. Greta, with no time to shut her door, dodged into the dark.

After Patty slammed into her bedroom, Greta watched her father at the table. He hunched over as if a weight pressed down on him. Then anger devoured any pity she felt. Why didn't he stand up to Patty? Would he actually consider leaving them? A solid assurance moved over her, then a sense of relief that Patty might actually be the one to go.

But by the time she finished in the bathroom and crawled into bed, the feeling of assurance had thinning spots. Then it became so transparent that Greta couldn't sleep, terror standing just behind it—in eight years, Dictator Patty had never, ever lost a battle.

Greta hardly slept. With every creak, she pictured Roger and Patty sneaking out, dragging luggage behind them. Once she even crept from bed and flung the door open, only to find a dark, empty hallway. Then she noticed the noise was coming from above, their landlord walking across the floor of the upstairs suite. She stood with her head against Ash's door, not sure if she should wake him. A draft moved over her legs, as if a window was open somewhere. Was she overreacting? Had she misunderstood? She crawled back under the blankets, waiting for her alarm.

When morning came—still black in January—Greta listened for the clatter of Roger and Patty in the kitchen. She could piece together their conversation by Patty's voice alone, clear above any kitchen appliance, including the blender. Nothing about leaving.

She waited until she heard Ash's door open. "Ash," Greta hissed as he headed for the bathroom. "Come here!"

He blinked, drowsy. "What?"

"Get in here." She dragged him through her door and eased it shut. While he stood there, his eyebrows pressed the wrong way from sleeping, she told him what she'd heard the night before. With every word, she felt more stupid. "What do you think that means?" She looked away to avoid his deadpan stare.

Ash didn't answer for a minute. Then, "Are you sure?"

"Well, yes. No. I think so," she said. "I heard it. But does it mean what I think it does?"

"Dad leave us?" He let out a long breath. "How—?" He stopped and shook his head. "No, he wouldn't."

It's what she wanted to hear, but the dismissal was irritating. "Fine," she said, pushing him toward the door, "but don't be surprised if we come home one day and he's gone."

Ash walked to the bathroom without looking back.

. . . .

In biology class Greta found herself watching the back of Rachel's long black layers. Every few minutes, Rachel ran her fingers through her hair, an absentminded compulsion. Greta remembered her doing the same when they'd watched Matt and Dylan's basketball games, especially when the score was close. Rachel's elbow would bump Greta's shoulder, her fingers working through those long strands again and again.

Rachel. Every time Greta saw her, she fought the urge to either slap her or apologize. Greta had had it all and lost it. And Rachel was there for the whole thing. Two more weeks in this term. Greta couldn't take any more sick days and still pass her classes. Two more weeks, then exams, then something new. *Please, something new.*

TWO

It felt weird walking home without Ash. Greta had hovered outside his math classroom while he finished an exam, before finally giving up and catching a bus alone. An old woman with a knitted scarf sat next to her, and Greta felt a breeze every time the woman coughed. Greta pictured her white blood cells rushing to meet the invasion. But at least the woman got the seat and not the college-age guy standing next to them in the aisle, glancing in her direction. Greta knew how carefully she'd have to hold her body if he sat next to her, so her thigh and arm wouldn't bump against his. She zipped her parka higher and tucked her chin inside.

As the bus rolled toward her stop, Greta rang the bell, stood and dodged to avoid brushing against him as she moved closer to the exit. On the sidewalk she paused, waiting to see his shadow behind her. He didn't get off. She exhaled. The air stilled for a moment, the cold fresh in her chest after the drafty heat of the bus, which made her body sweat while her feet went numb. Then the wind whipped her, stinging her eyes.

Their neighbor had already parked his Volvo across the street, a skiff of snow collecting on the windshield. He was nowhere to be seen. Greta fumbled for the key, her fingers slow and stiff. The air inside the basement suite was a relief for just a second, then registered as cold enough to leave her coat on. In the kitchen she reached for the box of matches in the cupboard above the stove. Pulling open the oven door, she turned on the gas and held the match close. Her hand jerked away as the flame ignited. She secretly feared a fireball that would take off her eyebrows. It was Ash who thought of using the oven as a heat source when the furnace still hadn't kicked in by October and the landlord upstairs never answered when they knocked. The landlord controlled the heat for the base-ment suite as well, which, Patty announced loudly—on a daily basis—was illegal.

Greta dragged a kitchen chair across the pocked hard-wood, parking it in front of the open oven door. The heat teased—welcoming in the front while the cold attacked from every other angle. She stood up to get a blanket.

At the mouth of the hallway, Greta stopped. A light under her dad and Patty's door. Someone was home? Maybe it had been left on by accident. The sun had dropped low, and the strip of light from the bedroom glowed in the dusky hall. Patty was almost never there when they got home from school, and Roger wouldn't be home from his daily run between Edmonton and Calgary until after six o'clock.

Greta leaned against the door, listening. Nothing. As she turned the knob in her hand, she heard a *clink* from inside, like one dish bumping another. Probably Patty. No need to wake the beast. Strange though. The smell of smoke, matches, candles. She cracked the door open an inch. Patty stood with her back to Greta, in front of a vanity against the opposite wall. Greta could see Patty's face reflected in the mirror, bent over a lit candle on a plate, her eyes two dark holes. *Probably prepping for a child sacrifice.*

Greta started to pull the door shut, then stopped. She recognized the tattered shoebox on the vanity, having sifted through it a million times herself. It held photos—old school pictures, family snapshots—the only ones not trapped on long-lost hard drives. She waited. Patty picked through them and held one away from her face to see it better, like she always did when she forgot her glasses.

Then she held it above the flame. Greta gasped and let the door fall open. The picture caught fire, curling and blistering at the corner. Patty's eyes met hers in the reflection—a skull in the dark room and candlelight. She stiffened and dropped the photo to the carpet, stamping out the flame with her foot.

"What are you doing?" Greta scrambled over the bed to reach it.

Patty bent down at the same time, but Greta pushed her arm away. It was a picture of her mother, Diana, with the same chestnut hair and green eyes as her twins. Greta had seen the photo, taken before a Christmas party, a hundred times before. Her mom was smiling, wearing earrings the shape of reindeer. It was Before Mother. Before breast cancer. Before her beautiful hair fell out. Before pain changed her face.

Before her body wasted. Greta remembered patting her mother's leg under the hospital sheet. There was nothing but bone and waxy skin left, not like a living person. Not the same mother. Before Mother and After Mother.

So many times, memories of After Mother drowned out the others. Memories of her gasping for some relief Greta couldn't bring. She had failed that mother—failed to save her, failed to make her smile, to distract her with pictures, crafts, teddy bears. Already gone, the mother she had known for eight years. Now Patty had burned a picture of Before Mother, a picture that was the only way Greta could remember her some days. The flame had eaten into her face before Patty stamped it out. Half her chin, one eye and one reindeer earring remained. Her smile gone.

Greta staggered to her feet, arms reaching for Patty. Patty stumbled back into the vanity, bumping it hard. The candle swayed and tipped on the plate, into the ashes of other pictures. There were more. More.

Greta choked on every ugly thought, every ugly feeling she'd ever had about Patty. She reached for the worst words, the ones that destroy, but only ended up with a growling in her throat. No escape—no way for Patty to get away from her. Patty cowered against the wall.

"I'm sorry," Patty sputtered. "It's like she's always here. You can't imagine."

Then she couldn't speak, as Greta's forearm pressed against her throat. Patty's bones against her skin, so frail. Why hadn't Greta seen it before? She'd grown tall, strong.

Patty was puny, weak. Greta could break her. Patty clawed at Greta's arm, pushed at her face. She was nothing at all.

"Greta." Ash wrenched her away. Patty gasped for air and slumped against the wall.

"She..." Greta couldn't say more.

"Just come. Come out of here." Darkness had overtaken the room now. Ash put an arm around her shoulder and pulled her away. His eyes shone round, black, like a crow's. The candle still burned on its side, drops of red wax hardening on the plate. A grotesque holiday craft.

Greta broke free to snatch the box off the vanity before letting Ash guide her to the door. She couldn't look back, not at any of it. The burned ashes of Before Mother, another life. Patty, pathetic and wheezing.

Ash led Greta to her room and shut the door. She fell on the bed, vomit working up her throat, tears scalding her face. The feeling of Patty's tiny bones still pressed into her arm. Pointing at the box, Greta tried to speak, but Ash said, "Shh. Not now." He sat near her feet. She wanted to check the box but found she couldn't move. What if there were no more photos? Would she kill Patty in cold blood?

They sat for half an hour, until the furniture turned to darkened shapes around them. Only the sound of their breathing. Outside her bedroom, not even a creak of the floor. Now she felt the steady draft from the window above her. Rolled in her blanket, Greta concentrated on breathing in and out. Then she found her voice to tell Ash what had happened.

Greta could feel anger bristling from him before he even spoke. He said, "She was lucky it was you."

Ash turned on a lamp on her nightstand and picked up the box. Sitting cross-legged on the floor with his back to Greta, he examined each picture. From her blanket cocoon she watched his long neck tilt down, his head shift from the box to each photo. It took a long time.

They heard the back door open, then Roger's and Patty's voices. Ash gathered the sloping pile of photos and dropped them back in the box, some spilling over the sides to the floor. Roughly he shoved it all under the bed and stood in front of her.

"There are three left." Ash's long arms, hanging near Greta's eyes, trembled. His fingers curled in, rolling tightly into fists.

She felt sick again. A lifetime in pictures—all that remained of that life—and only three had survived. She couldn't ask Ash which ones. What if one was a group shot, her mom's blurry head half covered by another? Or one of her arm and shoulder as she dangled a baby over an inflatable swimming pool? If Ash left to rough up Patty, she wouldn't move to stop him. She pressed her face into the pillow. "I..." She started to say *I hate her*, but the words seemed useless, inadequate to describe the monster clawing at her insides.

"It ends now. It's us or her." Ash turned and walked out the door, closing it behind him.

Greta let him go fight the battle. She didn't know herself what she might say or do. No boundaries anymore.

Patty shouted once, but Roger's and Ash's voices stayed low. Greta expected something more, like furniture being tossed or full-on wrestling. Ash came back after a few minutes, some tension gone from his face.

"Dad knows it all. It's in his hands now," Ash said.

The bedroom door next to them slammed, and then Patty started screaming about his children being killers and maniacs. This time Roger shouted back, maybe at seeing the candle and ashes: What right did she have to destroy something that wasn't hers? She'd gone too far. *Tell her, Dad.* Then Patty accused him of loving his dead wife more than her. *Damn straight.* Roger went on for a while about that not being true. *Puke.* After that their voices dropped low. Greta crept out once to use the bathroom but couldn't hear them anymore. Their light was still shining under the door.

Ash sat on the end of her bed and listened until Roger and Patty went quiet, the veins pulsing in his neck. When he stood to leave, Greta asked, "Ash, can you stay?" Even with her, Ash so easily became a shadow. "Please."

He paused for a second and then nodded. After making a trip for blankets and a pillow, Ash brought back a package of Patty's favorite cookies, which they were never allowed to touch.

"Eat up." He dropped them on her bed.

They ate every cookie. Ash smiled while he chewed, like he was personally swallowing all of Patty's hopes and dreams. Then came the wait. It felt like the time their mom had a biopsy on her tumor and they had to wait for results.

Whether positive or negative, the results would change everything from that point on. Good news would make life clear—they'd never spend another second being sad or fighting over the TV remote. Bad news would twist them all into something unrecognizable—characters in a tragic story that happens to other people.

"If they call a family meeting," Greta told Ash, "I'm not going."

But they didn't call a family meeting. Nor did Roger come to her room, apologizing or babbling in rage. He must have seen the burned photos of Diana. He used to tell Greta and Ash the story of how he'd chased her—the trucker who fell in love with the hippie. They seemed mismatched in every way. Diana was even an inch taller than him. It took him three years to show her that they worked. Ten years of marriage and two children. He fell to pieces when she died. What was he saying to Patty behind that door?

"What did Dad do when you told him?" Greta asked after they had turned off the light, Ash on the floor beside her bed.

He thought for a second. "He looked mad, but he didn't say much. Not when I was there anyway."

She drifted off but woke frequently—listening, waiting. What would Roger decide in the morning, Patty or them? She stared at the dim circle of her ceiling light at 3:00 AM and knew Ash was awake too. His breath made no sound, shallow in his chest. Neither of them spoke.

Her alarm jolted her awake at 6:30 AM. For one second it was just another morning. Then the memory rolled over her.

Ash shut off the alarm before she could. Had he slept at all? He stood, still wearing a rumpled black T-shirt and jeans, and waited for her to pull herself out of bed. She hovered at his shoulder as they walked to the door. When he pulled it open, she reached for his hand and squeezed it tightly. The first day of kindergarten all over again. As the cooler air of the hallway touched her skin, Greta fought the urge to retreat, slam the door, roll up in the blanket again. She wasn't ready for the results.

Ash motioned her past their door, to the living room and kitchen first. A strip of sky, as dark as the middle of the night, showed through the low basement windows. Greta felt the cold on her bare arms, an icy hand pressed there, but her body disconnected from it. Smoke hung in the air. Greta could sense the ghost of Patty, leaning against the doorframe with a cigarette between her fingers, flicking ashes through the open crack.

Greta led the way back to Roger and Patty's door. She examined it, but the varnished wood gave no clues. Ash stepped beside her and knocked. They waited five seconds. Ten seconds. Twenty seconds. He knocked again. Still nothing. He swung the door open. No one. The bed was unmade, with two dents in the pillows and the blanket twisted in a knot at the foot.

They stepped inside. All normal, except that Patty and Roger weren't usually gone by 6:00 AM. Especially Patty. Something else seemed off too. Greta ran her finger over the vanity where the plate and candle had stood. Despite the unmade bed, it looked too tidy. No—bare. It looked bare. She pulled open the dresser drawers. Not quite empty, but nearly. Some panty hose and summer shorts left behind.

"Ash, the closet." He swung open the door and pawed through the hangers. The same. Roger's suit still hung there, and a dress Patty wore once to a wedding.

The results. She couldn't look at Ash.

In eight years, Dictator Patty had never, ever lost a battle.

THREE

"I did something," Ash said. Greta opened her door in the morning and he filled the frame, like he'd been standing there all night.

"You're a little creepy sometimes, Ash. What have you done?" They had waited a day to see if Roger and Patty would miraculously reappear. They hadn't.

"You know how you told me a couple of weeks ago you thought Dad might take off?"

"And you didn't believe me?"

Ash's head dropped to his chest. "Well, I didn't want to believe you."

She hadn't wanted to believe it either. Behind Ash Roger and Patty's bedroom door hung ajar, a dark space. "Anyway. What did you do?"

"I put one of those locator apps on Dad's phone when he left it charging on the counter."

She let this sink in. "You're saying we can find out where Dad is."

Ash nodded. "If he hasn't discovered it already. It's in his app folder, but he doesn't go in there a lot. We'll be able to use your phone to find out their location."

Greta turned to grab her phone but swiveled back around. "Why didn't you tell me this yesterday?" It took him all night, standing outside her door?

He sighed. "It's stupid, but I thought they might come back on their own."

"Yes, that is stupid!" Snatching her phone off the dresser, she sat on the edge of the bed.

Ash came in and sat next to her, peering at the screen. "Take it easy. I'm telling you now, aren't I?" Greta opened the app folder. "I can do it," Ash said, reaching for the phone.

"I'll do it," Greta said, gripping the cracked screen. She pressed on the app and selected Roger's phone, the only choice listed. "They're in"—Greta squinted at the map—"White-court?" The smallest feeling of relief. They were in a place with a name, in the same province. A fixed point on a map.

Ash took the phone from her hands to look for himself. "That's a couple of hours northwest of here."

"Should I tell him we know where they are?" Greta asked. She had already called and texted him at least ten times— **Where are you? When are you coming home?**—and he hadn't replied or picked up.

Ash shook his head. "They might take off. We'll have a better chance face-to-face."

"How do we see him face-to-face? Aunt Lori's in Arizona until the end of March, so she can't drive us." They sat on the bed, looking ahead at nothing. "The bus. Do you have any money?"

"I have about a hundred bucks left from cutting lawns all summer," Ash said.

"I have twenty."

They reclined against the wall, their heads bumping to see better as Greta brought up the bus website. She typed in the leaving-from and going-to information.

"There's one leaving this afternoon." Greta saw it first. "You're right—about two hours each way."

Ash pulled the phone from her hands. "It would take almost all our money for both of us to go there and back."

"What if he leaves before we get there? We need a car," Greta said. "Is there even the slightest chance we could rent one?"

"Being under eighteen, only having our learner's permits, no credit card and a hundred and twenty bucks between us? No chance at all." Ash dropped the phone on the bed and sighed. "I guess we take the bus."

"Do we have any friends who drive?"

Ash gave her a look. "Do we have any friends?"

Greta shook her head. "I can't think of anyone."

She stood up and moved toward the shower. "Okay, you and I both come down with the stomach flu at lunchtime and leave. That will give us an hour to get to the bus depot and buy tickets." Standing in the doorway, she turned back to Ash. "There is someone."

"Who?"

She drew a deep breath, procrastinating. "Our neighbor across the street—that guy from your English class." She felt a stab of anxiety at the thought of being trapped in the car with him—a stranger—but then reminded herself that Ash would be with her. She didn't take back the words.

"We don't know that guy!" Ash protested.

"No," she said. "No, we don't, but it seems like he's always trying to get to know us. And I bet he'd do it for half the money. We could offer him fifty bucks."

"*Could you skip school to drive us—total strangers—to Whitecourt and back for fifty bucks?*"

"Well, yeah. Pretty much."

"There's no way he'll say yes."

"Then we're right back where we are now. We have nothing to lose."

Ash shook his head.

"I'll do it," Greta said. "I'm going to take a shower, get looking human and go knock on his door in half an hour." She'd stand on the porch, out in the open, and say no if he asked her inside.

"I'm not sending you by yourself." He sighed. "Fine."

Fifteen minutes before Ash and Greta normally left to catch the bus, they stood on their neighbor's porch across the street. His house looked like a better-kept version of theirs, with no basement suite. Their shoes left tracks in the icing-sugar snow that had fallen overnight, revealing the brown paint of the porch steps. Ash rang the doorbell and stepped back behind Greta's shoulder.

A man—probably the guy's dad—answered the door. Greta struggled for words. They hadn't factored in parents. He looked like he should star in a *How to Be a Lumberjack* video, or at least be wearing a kilt and tossing a caber or two. He had a bushy red beard and ruddy cheeks, with a bathrobe pulled tight around his wide chest.

"Yes?" He leaned out the door and looked back and forth between Greta and Ash.

Ash spoke first. "Is your...son...here?"

Please don't say, "Which one?"

"Yes." He didn't budge from the doorway. "And you are...?"

Greta found her voice. "We're your neighbors from across the street." She pointed over her shoulder. "We all go to the same school." *And pretty much ignore your son's daily attempts to make friends.*

"Hmm. Right. Okay." He leaned back and called, "Nate, your friends are at the door!"

Nate—the ginger with the Volvo—appeared behind his dad. He had a toothbrush in his mouth, spittle in one corner. He held up a finger for them to wait and ducked out of sight. His dad turned and disappeared into another room too, leaving Greta to prop open the screen door with her foot. Patty hated it when they did that—"heating the outdoors," she called it.

"Hey, guys." Nate was back again, a little red in the face. He regarded them on the porch, obviously confused. "I'm Nate, by the way. Well, it's Nathaniel, but I go by Nate."

"I'm Greta," she said, "and this is Ash." She glanced at Ash, wondering if he was going to confess that his name was Ashwin but he went by Ash. Nope. "Can we talk outside for a minute?" She gave him her best *we're-not-psychopaths* smile.

"Uh, sure." Nate pulled a coat off a hook and slipped on a pair of massive Sorels from a muddy mat. Probably his dad's.

Ash backed all the way down the steps, but Nate stopped right outside the door and waited. Greta stood next to him, suddenly feeling like the village idiot. *Who does this?*

"Our dad is married to this woman—" she began.

"*Woman* is being generous," Ash said. "Picture a wraith—bony, hideous."

Greta shot him a look. "Um...so we've had some problems with her and my dad"—she inhaled—"and *something* happened."

Nate leaned forward, waiting for the next word to fall.

Ash was right. Worst idea ever.

Ash stepped up beside Greta and gave her a look this time. "Basically, our dad took off with our stepmother, leaving us behind. We found out they're in Whitecourt, and we need a ride up there to try to talk him into coming back home. We can pay you fifty bucks. Interested?"

Nate's face relaxed. It was starting to look painful, the way his nearly-not-there eyebrows pinched together. "Oh, right." He let out a puff of air.

"You'd have to miss school," Greta said. "The sooner we leave, the better."

"I'm up for anything that involves missing school." Nate tapped his fingers against his legs. "Let me ask my dad."

"Well—" Ash raised his arm to protest. A well-meaning parent could blow this thing up fifty different ways. "Is there any way you could not quite tell the *whole* truth?" he asked. "We're trying to keep this quiet for now."

Nate stared for a full minute before nodding slowly, his mouth working like he was sucking on a marble. "I don't normally lie to my dad, but I get it. I'll come up with something." Then he disappeared again, leaving them on the porch. Greta bent her head toward the door but couldn't hear anything from inside. Ash scuffed the thin dust of snow with his toe, making it into a tornado shape before kicking it aside.

After a few minutes Nate cracked the door open and leaned out, the way his dad had before. "He said it's okay. I'll be ready in five minutes." Then he shut the door and left them standing there.

"Okaaaaaay?" Ash said.

"Okay! Let's get ready!" Greta nearly leaped off the porch and bolted back to the basement suite. They grabbed a couple of water bottles and stuffed granola bars in their pockets. Ash pulled his money from a margarine container in the storage room—fifty for Nate and an extra ten just in case. A motor of anxiety pushed Greta along, like her worry could move them closer, faster.

When they went back outside, Nate was already chiseling ice from his windshield through a cloud of exhaust. "Rebus doesn't like the cold much," he said, running the scraper along each wiper blade.

Greta thought for a second he meant his dad—the lumberjack—and then realized Nate had named his car Rebus. Beside her, Ash pinned her with a stare. It was going to be a long four hours.

Nate manually unlocked the passenger door and held it open. Greta flipped the front seat forward and climbed into the back. Ash started to fold his long body in beside her, his neck bent at an unnatural angle. Greta hissed, "Get up front! This isn't a taxi!"

He mouthed back, *You go up front then*, gesticulating between her and Nate.

"You're...a boy...and in the same class." Realizing how lame that sounded, she added, "I'll do the way back." Greta hoped that Nate, still standing by the open door, hadn't heard.

Ash pinched his lips tight and gave her a murderous look. He unfolded his body and slid into the front seat instead. Nate shut the door and moved toward the driver's side.

"I hate you," Ash whispered.

Greta smiled into her collar. *This should be interesting.*

Despite the heat blowing at maximum, the seat beneath her radiated cold. A pine-tree air freshener dangled from the rearview mirror. The interior—mostly red plush and duct tape—was immaculately clean.

Nate backed the car out of the driveway and headed toward a four-way stop. "Not gonna lie," he said. "These tires are pretty bald. I'll show you." He accelerated, then slammed on his brakes. The car fishtailed and slid to a stop at an angle, the back tire bumping the curb.

Ash didn't speak but hunched his shoulders a little higher. Greta heard him loud and clear. *I hate you. I hate you. I hate you.*

"I'm almost on empty. Do you have a twenty on you?" Nate asked Ash.

Ash nodded and dug in his pocket. They pulled into a gas station a few blocks away. When Nate stepped out to pump gas, closing the door behind him, Ash turned to face Greta in the back seat.

"Not too late to back out and take the good ol' Greyhound with its not-bald tires. And psychologically sound driver."

"There is something a little 'stranger danger' about him."

Ash turned back to face the windshield. "He's the type of guy who'd either give you his last five bucks to buy lunch *or* giggle maniacally as he cut off your legs with a hacksaw. And not much in between."

Nate slid back into his seat and smiled at them. "Okay. Brace yourselves. Rebus hasn't gone highway speeds for a while."

"Why did you name him…uh, her…Rebus?" Greta said.

"I don't know." Nate shrugged. "He just kind of looked like a Rebus."

So yellow Volvos from the eighties are male and named Rebus. They headed out of the city in total silence. Ash looked up the route on Google Maps and prompted Nate when and where to turn. They were driving through Spruce Grove—a small city right outside Edmonton—before anyone spoke again.

"What did you tell your dad?" Greta asked Nate.

"I told him you guys needed a ride and moral support to get some testing done at a clinic."

"Testing? What kind of testing?" Ash sat up straight, his eyes bugging like Nate's.

"I was deliberately vague." Nate cleared his throat. "I may have implied it would be embarrassing for you if I shared more."

A damp, dirty feeling settled over Greta, catching her off guard.

Ash's face turned purple. "Why," he sputtered, "why would you say that?"

Nate swallowed and glanced between Ash and the road. "Look, I'm sorry. It was the only explanation I could think of where he would let me miss school and wouldn't offer to take you himself."

Ash rubbed his eyes and turned to face the window. "Yeah, okay. I just…" He trailed off.

"It worked, didn't it?" Nate asked.

Point taken.

Greta tried to clear a path through the feeling she had, tried to find some logic. "Yes, Nate. It worked," she said. Let the lumberjack think she was pregnant, an addict or had an STI. They were in a car on their way to Whitecourt, weren't they? "And we're grateful."

Nate nodded and smiled at her in the rearview mirror. "That's all right. I've been wanting to meet you guys for a while now."

And we've been trying to avoid you for a while now. Greta broke eye contact to look out the window, feeling guilty. Did Ash feel it too? The back of his head gave away nothing more than hunched misery.

"You'll need to watch for the Highway 43 exit," Ash said, gesturing to the right. "After that we'll eventually hit Whitecourt."

After a few more minutes they turned off Highway 16 onto 43, narrow and hilly. Greta watched the farmland and fence posts, broken by patches of poplars, their spotted trunks almost blending into the snow. Pickup trucks—and even the odd blue-haired grandma—ripped past them on the highway. Greta strained against her lap belt to check the speedometer. Ninety kilometers per hour.

"I think you can go at least a hundred here, Nate. Maybe even 110."

Nate shook his head. "Rebus starts to shake over ninety." He accelerated, and the steering wheel vibrated in his hands until he dropped back to ninety. Greta quashed the bubble of impatience rising inside her. Was this better than the bus?

Nate talked—for a long time—about alternative bands from the nineties and how hard it was to find stores that carried the cassette tapes he needed for Rebus. Ash leaned back against the headrest and closed his eyes; Greta could tell he wasn't really sleeping by the way his head didn't roll with the movement of the car.

They passed by some small towns. "Sangudo," Nate said at the latest one. "That one's fun to say. Try it. San—goo—do."

Greta said it just to humor him, especially given Ash's *I'm asleep* routine. Maybe it was a little fun. They crossed over a river, frozen and piled with snow. On road signs the kilometers to Whitecourt slowly, painfully decreased. Farmland gave way to forest. She forgot where they were going for a minute, craning to see the sway of old pines, their branches caked in white. The glaring sun of early morning shifted to a matted gray. Nate continued talking. About what, Greta didn't know.

With nothing to do but watch pine trees and sky, Greta thought about *them*, about when things were good. She'd been at West Edmonton High for almost two months when Rachel spoke to her for the first time. Greta had been assigned to Rachel's biology group, along with a girl named Priya and a guy named Scott, who never spoke. They sat on stools around a table the shape of a kidney bean, with a poster of a uterus on the wall and a pickled tapeworm in a jar beneath it. Rachel and Priya were talking about their Halloween costumes. They were dressing up as the Spice Girls with two other girls, Samantha, or "Sam," and Chloe.

"We just need Sporty Spice now," Priya said. "Then we have all five."

Greta was the only one actually doing the biology worksheet. *Pulmonary artery: carries deoxygenated blood from the right ventricle to the lungs.* It helped, being good at school. It distracted her from how lonely she'd been since the beginning of September.

"What about you, uh, Gwen?" Rachel asked, really looking at Greta for the first time. Priya shot Rachel a warning look for fraternizing with the enemy—one of the "unspecials."

"It's Greta. Sorry, what?"

Rachel ignored Priya. "What are you doing for Halloween? We're going as the Spice Girls and need a Sporty Spice. You're tall and, you know, athletic."

Greta knew she looked the part. She'd grown two inches over the past year, and people always asked her if she played basketball. Probably neither Rachel nor her friends wanted to be stuck wearing sweats and runners on Halloween. And Greta was a safe bet, being new. No embarrassing ex-boyfriend or awkward yearbook photo to hold against her.

"I...uh...I'm not sure yet." Actually, she had planned on staying home with Ash and handing out Halloween candy. Hoarding all the Snickers bars.

"You should join our group. We're dressing up for school, and there's a party that night."

Greta started to say no, but for what? To keep eating lunch alone, checking dark corners for Ash? "Well, maybe. I don't think I have the right clothes though." Definitely no sexy workout wear in her closet.

"I can lend you something," Rachel said. She was slim, Asian and several inches shorter than Greta.

"Uh..."

"Come over after school tomorrow, and we'll figure it out."

Greta had met the whole group at Rachel's house the next day and ended up taking home a skin-tight tank top of

Rachel's and a pair of yoga pants that didn't fit Sam anymore. On Halloween day, Rachel dressed up as Posh Spice. Priya, with her untamable black hair and Cleopatra eyeliner, was appropriately Scary Spice. Blond, curly-haired Sam was Baby Spice. She had a wide, friendly face. Big bones, as Patty would say. Chloe—Ginger Spice—sprayed red streaks in her hair and giggled a lot without making eye contact. Greta floated on their high through the hallways and cafeteria, others stopping them constantly for pictures and selfies.

That night Rachel picked her up and drove her to a party at Priya's house, which looked like the boss of show homes. Priya answered the door, taking their coats and laying them across a nearby bench. Shiny wood floors, pristine furniture, vases, original pieces of art on the walls.

"Don't touch anything," Priya said to her. "My parents are gone until tomorrow, and they don't know I'm having a party."

Rachel rolled her eyes as soon as Priya turned her back. "Yeah, Greta," she whispered when Priya stepped down a staircase to the basement, "try not to wreck the house." Greta stifled a laugh.

The house had caught her off guard. Also, Greta had imagined something different when Rachel said "Halloween party," like the ones in movies—pounding bass, a crush of drunken people dancing and wandering around in elaborate costumes, strobe lights. Greta had thought she would wander around, too, get lost in all the noise or find a quiet corner. In reality, a few people sat on couches arranged in a square in the middle of the room. The ceiling was low, lit by pot lights, and Greta saw the outline of a pool table off in a darkened corner. A phone and wireless speaker on the coffee table played music. It was super low-key. Other than the Spice Girls, no one wore a costume. Greta paused at the foot of the stairs, but Priya and Rachel marched ahead. She followed.

Rachel stepped up like it was her house. "Everyone, this is Greta. She's our Sporty Spice." She smiled at Greta and started naming and pointing to people. As she talked a short, muscly blond guy walked over and put his arm around her waist. No, right on her butt. "This is Matt, my boyfriend," Rachel said. She gave him a coy smile. Yup, still on her butt.

Besides Priya and Sam, who stood behind a couch, talking to a girl called Angela, there was Matt—the butt groper—a guy named Dylan who had sat at their table at lunchtime, and someone named Angus with chin-length dreads.

As though reading Greta's mind, Priya said, "More people are coming later."

Greta sat on the empty leather couch in front of Priya, Sam and Angela. Rachel went over to a bar by the pool table and brought Greta back an orange drink that smelled like nail polish remover. Then she curled up on Matt's lap on another couch and whispered in his ear.

Across from Greta, Dylan sat alone. Greta tried not to stare at him—one of *those* people. She had noticed him at lunchtime too: dark, chin-length hair, almost the same color as hers, strong jaw, great smile. There was something friendly about his face. She wanted him to look at her.

Wanted him to like her. *Don't be such a cliché. Look at Angus instead, coming this way.* Angus smiled and sat next to her.

As they ran through a list of questions about who she was and where she'd gone to school before, Greta found her head turning toward Dylan. She caught his eye for a second. Was he looking at her too? Wasn't he? Angus noticed her eyeing Dylan and trailed off mid-question. Then Angela came up behind Dylan, bent over and draped her arms around his neck. Her copper-red hair fell over his shoulders. She had a heart-shaped face and perfect skin. Greta snapped her head away, her face warm. The drink, which kind of burned, didn't help. She tipped the bottom up and finished the last of it. "Sorry, what were you saying?" she said to Angus.

Sam saved her by calling up all the Spice Girls, minus Chloe, to lip-synch "Wannabe." Greta butchered everything except the chorus, which made Dylan laugh. Was he watching her? When they finished, she stayed standing with Sam and Rachel.

"Angus seems to like you." Rachel gave her a conspiratorial smile over the rim of her plastic cup.

"He's, uh…nice. So are Angela and Dylan, like, together?"

Sam and Rachel snorted at the same time.

"What? Just curious. They're a nice, sort of…couple." She was becoming more stupid with every passing minute.

"Sweetie, with the exception of me, everyone wants to be with Dylan," Rachel said.

Greta looked away to hide her red cheeks and tried not to watch Angela rest her head on Dylan's chest. At the end of the night, though, he was there. Just the two of them as she collected her shoes and coat from the entryway. She stumbled as she bent for her shoes, still wobbly from the radioactive punch. He steadied her, a hand on each hip. She'd felt the warmth of his fingers through her Sporty Spice yoga pants, her heart hammering as he smiled down on her. "You okay?" he asked.

"Just a little dizzy."

"I've got you," he said. On one level, Greta had hoped Angela hadn't heard that. On another, she hadn't cared at all. Then he'd let go, smiling over his shoulder as Matt called him away.

That was all before the cabin. Greta shifted in her duct-taped seat in the back of Rebus, not wanting to think about after.

FOUR

Rebus started to shake at ninety, so Nate dropped to eighty-five. Pickups followed with their headlights nearly touching Rebus's bumper before tearing past, their tires spitting gravel at Nate's windshield. Greta bit back her impatience again, grinding her teeth together. Roger and Patty could be hours away by now. She slid the phone off the edge of Ash's seat and tried the locator app again. Still in Whitecourt. She took some slow breaths.

Finally. *Welcome to Whitecourt* on an official sign. Greta unbuckled her suffocating seat belt and tapped Ash on the shoulder. He opened his eyes immediately. *Sleep liar.*

She waved the phone in front of him. "Ash, we're here. Let's see where Dad is."

Nate pulled off to the side of the road, and all three heads converged on the screen. "It looks like they're close," Ash said. He used two fingers to zoom in. "Yes, the second right."

A lump hardened in Greta's throat. *It's now.* Nate drove slowly—to the point of torture—to make sure they took the right turn. On either side of them hotels, motels, fast-food and family restaurants. Parking lots full of pickups and semis hauling strange equipment.

"It's there. Dad's truck." She saw it first, "bobtailing," as Roger called it—not pulling anything. It looked lonely in the motel parking lot, with only Patty's junkyard Honda parked nearby.

Nate pulled into an empty stall by the motel office. The Hideaway Motel.

"How do you know which room they're in?" Nate asked. They scanned the row of identical orange-painted doors for a clue. Nothing. Roger had parked his truck off to the side, not close to any door.

"I'll go in and ask," Greta said. No one protested. Ash always let her take on the situations needing a human touch, the same way she let him take on the showdowns with Patty. Their own unspoken strengths.

She took a deep breath and forced her face to relax before stepping through the door. A woman in her fifties sat behind the front desk, sifting through a stack of papers and receipts. It took Greta only a minute to explain she had come to meet her father, Roger Woods, but he hadn't said which room he was in. "He owns the big red truck." Greta pointed vaguely toward the door. Again with the *I'm-not-a-psychopath* smile.

The woman sat in front of a computer and moved the mouse around. "Yes, dear. It looks like he's in room ten."

"Thank you." Greta sighed as she said it, making the woman look up from her screen. "It's been a long drive.

Thanks." Then she backed out the door before the woman could ask any questions.

Ash climbed out of Rebus to meet her.

"Room ten," she said.

Nate unrolled his window as they started to walk away. "I'll wait here!" he called to their backs. Greta barely heard him, her eyes fixed on the silver 10 on the orange paint.

"What are we going to say to him?" Greta asked. "Why didn't we talk about this?"

"What is there to say?" Ash shrugged. "*Come home, you moron. Bring the Antichrist if you must.*"

She reached over and clutched his hand. That was happening a lot lately. There was a time he would've shaken her off, before everything got so twisted. She let go to pound on the door, filling her lungs and blowing the air out slowly. *This will work. It's got to work.*

A voice from inside, low. They were there. As Ash raised his hand to knock again, the door opened a crack. Roger's blue eye met theirs. *Dad.* If it'd been Patty, Gretta might've climbed back into Rebus and taken off.

"Dad." She said it out loud this time.

Roger let the door fall open, revealing an unmade bed and some shirts tossed over the back of a chair. The funky odor of weed hit them full on, making Ash and Greta flinch. Roger struggled to form words, something close to terror on his face.

"No, you're not hallucinating, Dad," Ash said. "We're your children—Ash and Greta. The ones you abandoned in Edmonton."

Greta stepped forward to hug him at the same time Patty came out of the bathroom. "What the hell?" she said, striding to the door. "What are you two doing here?"

"What are *you* two doing here!" Ash barked, pointing at Roger and Patty.

Greta grabbed Ash's arm to rein him in. "Dad, we want you to come home. We can work this out."

"No," Patty whispered, and then she shouted, "No!" She looked at Greta. "*You* tried to kill me!" Then to Ash. "And *you* tried to force him to leave me! I'm done with both of you."

"Dad." Greta attempted to block the force of Hurricane Patty. "Can we talk for a minute?"

Roger blinked, his eyes glassy, unfocused. His face shifted from confusion to anguish. "I'm trying to work some things out with Patty. I'll be home soon, okay?" He smacked his lips together and swallowed.

"He will *not* be home soon," Patty said, wrenching Roger's shoulder away from the door and starting to close it. "Now get out of here!"

"I'll send you some—" Roger began.

"No money! You're on your own!"

Ash stuck his foot in the door as Patty slammed it, Roger just a shadow in the background now. Patty kicked at Ash's toes, then stamped his boot with the heel of her bare foot. "Get out of here! You're not wanted!"

"Ash." Greta touched his hand. "Ash." She squeezed his icy fingers tightly. "Let it go."

He blocked her out, trying to wedge the door open, his eyes focused on the outline of Roger.

"Ash." She shook his hand, pinching tighter. "Ash."

At once he pulled his foot back, and the door banged shut. They stared at it, the silver 10 against the orange. The deadbolt clicked on the other side.

Then she felt it—the weight of desperation, three hours of hope and fear, the sting of every one of Patty's words. *You're not wanted.* The pathetic shadow of their father. It mingled in a cloud and lowered over her. She swayed, surprised to feel tears on her cheeks. Her legs too heavy to move.

"What a waste." Ash swore and kicked the white stucco wall. He pounded a fist against their window. "What a bloody waste!" He turned and saw Greta, eyes still fixed on the orange door.

"C'mon. Let's get out of here. If those are parents, who needs them? They suck. You suck!" he screamed at their closed door. "Let's go." He took her hand this time, like she was a two-year-old, and led her back to the car.

Nate's face was ghost white. "I'm sorry," he said, standing outside the car as they approached. "I wasn't sure if I should do something."

Ash shook his head and moved the seat for Greta to climb in. "Can I drive?" he asked Nate.

Nate looked a little distressed. "Uh, sure. You know about the speed thing, right?"

Ash snatched the key from Nate's barely extended hand and slid into the driver's seat as if it were his own car.

Nate climbed in on the passenger's side and buckled his seat belt. Ash started Rebus, wrenched it into reverse and peeled out of the parking lot, rubber spinning on ice.

"Whoa. A little slower," Nate said.

Ash signaled left and cut in front of oncoming traffic. Nate clutched the handhold on the door. The rear side of the *Welcome to Whitecourt* sign sprung up on their left.

"I think it's just sixty here," Nate said. He leaned over Ash to check the speedometer. "You're going at least eighty."

"You want to know the irony?" Ash's voice filled the whole car, drowning out the vibration of the steering wheel. "Before, Dad would've freaked out if he'd caught us smoking weed. *Oh, no! My precious babies are becoming addicts! They'll be selling their bodies for a fix in less than a month!*" He floored the gas pedal.

Nate's other hand gripped the bottom of his seat. Greta swayed in the back—no seat belt on.

"Higher than a kite, and he still can't stand up to her!" Ash swerved into the other lane to pass, cutting too close as he moved back. The car behind them honked; Ash unrolled the window and waved the finger.

"And what is *this*?" He gestured to two cars in front of them, side by side in the fast and slow lanes, going the same speed. He moved behind the one in the fast lane, gunning closer. "Move it, asshole!"

"Back off," Nate yelped.

The car signaled right and started crossing over to the slow lane. Ash swerved around it, hitting the rumble strips on the shoulder of the road before jerking back. Rebus's rear swayed, searching for traction, and then gripped the road again. They shot forward. Greta stopped breathing at all, everything moving in slow motion.

The whole car trembled, ripping past other vehicles.

"Pull over, now!" Nate shouted.

Ash snapped his head to the side to look at him, as if he suddenly remembered Nate was there. Their speed faltered.

"This is *my* car, and I want you to pull over!" Pink blotches covered Nate's paste-white face. He pointed to a roadside turnout ahead. "Right here! You hear me?"

Ash pursed his lips, cocked his head to the side and gunned it. The vibration swallowed every other sound as they sped toward the turnout. He took the exit fast and jammed his foot on the brake. The world swirled around them, beautiful.

This is how I die.

On Rebus's bald tires, the car ripped in a circle and a half before coming to a stop. They all sucked in a collective breath, now facing the highway they'd just left. Greta hugged the back of Nate's seat, her cheek pressed against the head-rest. The gearshift clunked as Ash shifted it into Park. He turned the key toward him. Rebus shuddered and fell silent. The only sound was Nate panting like a dog.

Ash closed his eyes and swallowed. He pulled the key from the ignition and offered it to Nate, his hand trembling. "I'm sorry."

Nate paused, then snatched the key away.

Ash gripped the steering wheel with both hands, his head drooping forward. "Damn him!" He beat his palm against the wheel. Then he opened the door and leaped out, falling against the hood of the car, scrambling to get his feet under him. Rebus rocked, convulsed.

"Hey!" Nate shouted, fumbling with his seat belt.

Ash strode to the outer edge of the rest stop, where pines rimmed the clear space. Combat boots flailing, he kicked a garbage can once, twice. It rolled on its side, spilling fast-food garbage into the snow. Greta could see the dent from where she sat, her nails squeezing half moons into her palms. The back of Nate's seat held her head upright. Another car pulled in behind them, idled for a second and then turned back to the highway.

Ash stopped and looked skyward, as if waiting for something. His breath billowed around him, like he'd just run a marathon. His black jacket slipped off his shoulders and his boot laces hung loose. Unraveling.

Nate opened his door and walked around to the driver's seat, leaving the passenger door hanging open. Any warmth was whisked away in one gust. A minute passed. Ash raked his hands through his hair and stumbled back to them. The whole car shuddered as he dropped into his seat—the heaviest person in the world.

Ash exhaled, expelling the last sliver of light in him. "He's dead to me." They waited for more. "Let's go."

Nate turned the key, and Rebus started—loyal, forgiving. They drove eighty on the highway, hazard lights blinking.

For the next hour Greta watched Ash absorb the weight of every particle around him. Rebus tilted lower on Ash's side—subtle but discernable. Greta buckled her seat belt to keep from sliding toward him, falling into his black hole. Dark matter. *Nonluminous.* This time Ash's head did loll from side to side with the movement of the car. It was as if he'd come back from the rest stop, buckled his seat belt and ceased to live.

Nate said, "I need to stop for gas," and Ash's long arm held out thirty dollars across the canyon of space between them.

They pulled into an Esso station in a hamlet called Gunn. When he got out to pump the gas, Greta and Ash sat in silence, not wanting to think past that moment. Heading home to a dark question mark.

Nate paid for the gas and climbed back in. "Here," he said, tossing a jumbo package of licorice into Ash's lap. "I only had five bucks left, so I got us something to share."

Greta saw Ash cock his head in her direction, ever so slightly.

. . . . .

"It's cold in here." Greta dragged her blanket into Ash's storage room and flopped onto a pile of discarded clothes lying on the floor beside his mattress. "Do you want me to light the oven?"

Ash lifted his head and then dropped it back on the pillow. He lay on top of the blankets, as if he had fallen on that very spot and was waiting for the earth to drift over him. She touched the bare skin of his arm. A cadaver.

"Ash, move. At least cover yourself." She tugged at the blanket under his body. He didn't shift to help her. She took half of her blanket and covered him with it.

This was worse, Ash like this. Worse than Patty and Roger high in an orange-painted dump in Whitecourt, driving around in his red truck, trying to forget two rocks left behind. Worse than the vibration of their slamming door still buzzing through her. Worse than the three-hour drive home in a barely heated Volvo. Worse than their thin "thank you" to Nate after nearly crashing his car, and the way he still managed to look sad for them at the end of it all. What was wrong with them? *Here you go—we'll pay you fifty bucks to nearly die.*

The cold. She'd felt it for so long now—hard to know when it even started. Something deep inside her clenched tight and trembled. Her toes, fingers aching numb for hours now. Her shoulders hunched up near her ears. She thought of the shower—at least fifteen good minutes of hot water before it would taper to a disappointing lukewarm. But then the frigid air would sting her the second her foot touched the bath mat, when the steam dissipated. Unbearable.

A weak whistle in the vents signaled the heat kicking in—the actual heat from the furnace. It couldn't touch her now; she was too far gone. Her body started shaking, accentuated by Ash's dead stillness. He didn't say anything, and she was grateful. She fell asleep curled up on his dirty laundry.

Ash was already awake when she opened her eyes. Greta could always tell when he wasn't sleeping. He lay on his back, watching the hint of morning through the open storage-room door. She twisted onto her back too, hiking the blanket up under her chin. The air attacked her exposed knee before she pulled it in.

Ash laced his fingers behind his head. "How come you don't seem that upset about Dad leaving?"

Greta always assumed she didn't have to explain with Ash. So disappointing, the times he proved her wrong. "You mean because I didn't nearly cause a five-car pileup and kick over a garbage can?"

Ash didn't respond.

"To be honest, I'm kind of in shock." What would happen the moment they left the storage room?

They let the silence sit.

"But I'm not surprised," Greta said. She felt Ash's head snap in her direction. "Deep down, it's what I thought would happen after I heard them talking." Her stomach growled. Every part of her felt achy and hollow. "Even if I hadn't heard them talking."

"We've lost them both," Ash said. Greta knew he didn't mean Patty. His words laid her flat. There was no way they'd ever climb out of the storage-room pit now.

"Yes."

Ash became so still, even breathing didn't move his body. *How does he do that?* Minutes passed.

"What do we do now?" Greta asked. She knew Ash was waiting for her to say it first.

His breath started again. "I guess we...get up. We go to school."

"Really?"

"Won't it be a red flag if we don't? They'll start calling home. Send social workers or something."

"They'll call us at home to tell us we weren't at school?"

"You know what I mean," he said. "We don't want any more problems."

Was this Ash speaking? He climbed out of bed, disturbing her pocket of warmth. Greta scrambled to cover the breach in the blanket. He turned his back to her and pulled his T-shirt off, picking a clean one from the shelf. Through the dim sunlight, she saw the old scar on his shoulder blade from a tree house nail. His jeans were wrinkled from sleeping in them, hanging low on his skinny hips.

Greta scoffed. "I think school is the least of our worries."

Ash pulled on the new shirt and tugged the silver chain hanging from the lightbulb. She winced, even though the wattage was pathetic. "Get up, Greta."

She pushed herself to her elbows, indignant. Then she saw his face, his jaw clenched but green eyes calm.

"From this point on, I look out for you, and you look out for me," Ash said. "Until Aunt Lori gets back from Arizona, we only have each other."

Ash was right—there were no other relatives in the picture. Roger's parents had died when Greta and Ash were three, and their mother's parents ran yoga retreats in Mexico. They couldn't stand Roger when Diana was still alive, and now

Ash and Greta were lucky to get the occasional Christmas card in the mail. Greta didn't even know how to reach them.

She flopped back onto the dirty laundry. School. Ash didn't know what it cost her, going there every day. She wanted him to know without her saying the words out loud. What relief, what terror that would be. And since Patty wasn't there to get annoyed about Greta being home during the day, or Roger to show mediocre interest in test scores, there was no reason anymore. Cut the whole thing loose and float away.

"There's one day left in the term. We get up. We go. Then we write our exams. And we keep going until we're done with that school and all of this." He motioned to the storage room around him, but Greta knew what he meant. *This*—this substandard life. The glint of anger returned to his eyes, and his chest puffed tighter against his shirt. "Get up, Greta. Please."

She reached out for him to pull her up. "Fine," she said, shaking his hand away the second her feet were under her. "I'll go, but you have to stick with me. Where do you go anyway? You want me to come and then can't get away fast enough."

Ash dropped his head. "I guess I always thought you were better off without me dragging you down. You stand a better chance of making friends on your own."

"Well," she said, furious at the tremor in her voice, "you can see how well that's working for me." *Tell him.*

Ash still didn't look up. "Yeah. Okay. Sorry."

She nodded, even though he couldn't see it. "You light the oven. I'm taking a shower." She stepped through the door.

FIVE

"We should apologize to him," Ash said, his shoulder against Greta's on the bus. The front door swiveled open for a new passenger, letting in a gust of frigid air. Greta turned her head away from a couple making out near the front of the bus, focusing on Ash's face instead. She zeroed in on a few strands of hair against his temple. *Brown, dark, brunette, chocolate.* She mentally listed off all the possible words for their coloring. *Eyelashes: jet-black, inky, coal colored.* Methodically Greta named every adjective she could think of, sucking in a breath to stave off that dizzy carsick feeling. Ash narrowed his eyes and watched her face. *What did he just say?* Right. Apologize. *To?* She looked around, still avoiding the front, like the one needing the apology was sitting beside them. Nate. Yes, Nate. Relief at being able to find the thread of conversation.

"*You* should apologize to him." His words, their conversation, kept her there with Ash, prevented her from sliding toward panic. They hadn't seen Nate in two days, either coming or going.

"Maybe you could make him cookies or something."

"*You* make him cookies," Greta said. "You did the crime; you do the time." It was a classic Rogerism, oddly satisfying to say. Out of the corner of her eye she saw the bus doors slide open and the couple slip off, dodging the line filing on. Greta relaxed back in her seat again.

She knew Ash wasn't trying to be a caveman, asking her to bake the cookies. They never talked about it, but Ash always used to bake with their mother. How many times had Greta seen him standing on a kitchen chair next to her, leveling a cup of flour with a butter knife? Or him guiding a mixer around a bowl, her hand clamped firmly on top of his? Greta had always darted in to stick her fingers in the batter, but Ash was methodical, almost scientific. Patty offered to bake with him once, before she and Roger got married. Ash just stood in the kitchen doorway and dropped his chin, his eyes still fixed on her. Like one of those psycho kids who's all quiet until he snaps and stabs someone with an apple corer. Now Greta only saw him wander in for crackers or to make macaroni and cheese.

Last day of the term. Greta paused outside her biology classroom and repeated those words in her head, wanting some comfort from them. One more class trapped in a room with Rachel and Priya, avoiding Priya's curious looks, watching Rachel avoid her. She should have sailed through the door. Instead, anxiety—like she'd swallowed a stick whole—jammed up her center, threatening to push everything up through her mouth. Ms. Nordstom, the teacher, stuck her head out to sweep the hallway with her eyes before closing the door.

"Ah, Greta. Come in."

The spell broke. Greta took a step forward and moved to her seat, her eyes fixed straight ahead. Her heart pounding as she moved to her seat, she never once turned to see if Rachel was even there. She saw the back of Priya's head near the front, but Priya didn't peer over at Greta today. Greta sat rigid in her chair and tried to focus on breathing, hearing only snatches of what Ms. Nordstrom said. *Last day of classes. Then exams. Then something new.*

When Ash appeared at her locker at lunchtime, she glowered at him. It was his fault she was there. Still, he hadn't taken off, and that counted for something. They ate in an empty classroom. Her body unclenched a little as they closed the door. Just the two of them in the quiet space.

At the end of the day Greta and Ash stepped through the front doors and headed to the bus stop, Greta checking around them constantly. The temperature had risen—she didn't shrink from the air like she had that morning. Snow, tinged gray, covered the green space in front of the school and the base of the flagpole. It hadn't snowed in a week. Sand had been scattered over the icy patches on the walkway.

The rush to get ready for school gone. The panic of having to see *them* gone. Just the bus carrying Ash and Greta to their empty home. Ash must have felt it too. They said nothing at all on the bus ride or the walk from their stop. Rebus was already parked outside Nate's house.

Greta waited until they had stepped inside, not wanting to say the words in the wide open. "We could check the app again, you know. Maybe they're closer to home now."

Ash kicked off his snowy shoes. "I told you. I don't have a father anymore, and I never had a stepmother." His words came out tight, clipped. "But I can't stop you from looking." He ducked through the storage-room door, still wearing his coat, and closed it behind him. His face had twitched when Greta suggested he move into Roger and Patty's room. She didn't blame him. She could still smell the candle and matches.

Greta lit the oven and grabbed a cheese slice from the fridge to prove to herself that she wasn't in a hurry. Then she settled at the kitchen table, the stick back in her throat again. They could be in Whitecourt or the Northwest Territories or even somewhere in the city. What would she do if the app showed her Edmonton? Hide in a bush near their hotel and try to catch Roger on his own?

The phone's battery showed 20 percent. Greta didn't tell Ash she'd checked for texts and missed calls every half hour since they got up that morning. She opened the app and held her breath, waiting for the results.

Nothing. Roger must have deleted it. Actually, Patty would've been the one to find and delete it. She was the more tech-savvy one and also the more suspicious one. That last tie to her father snipped clean. Ash was right—just the two of them now. A grim relief, the clarity of it.

While Ash slept, pouted—whatever he did in the storage room—Greta got to work. Half an hour later, she knocked on his door, calling him out. He followed her to the kitchen, raised his head and took a step back.

"This is all the food we have," she said, "not counting what's in the fridge. Which isn't much." She swept her arm across the cans of food, boxes of cereal and Jell-O packets spread over the countertop.

Panic on his face. Their food supply was finite; she felt it too. One day soon they would eat that last package of lime Jell-O, and then what?

"Soooo"—she drew out the word—"we need to talk about what's next."

Ash nodded.

"How much money do we have now?"

"Seventy dollars," he said, "including your twenty."

"Okay," she said. "That's not great."

"What about calling Aunt Lori?"

"In Arizona?"

"Sure. She'd help."

For a second, Greta felt the weight of their burden shift—less crushing. Then: "Dad had her number on his phone. Do you know it?"

Ash shook his head. Neither of them spoke for a minute. "We can both apply for jobs," he said.

"We don't have much time. February's rent is due in a week."

Ash's face looked grimmer, if that was possible.

"We could tell someone, ask for help. Like a teacher or someone at school," Greta said.

Greta could almost see the thoughts tumbling in his head. "What would happen then?" Ash asked.

She shrugged. Brand-new territory. What *would* happen to them, their home, their dad?

"Okay." He turned and fixed on her, something firmer in his face. "Okay. Let's look for work this week and see if we can do it on our own first."

Greta knew that even if they found jobs that week, they wouldn't get paid for a few weeks. And would it actually be enough for rent, food and bus passes? Still, it felt good to make a decision, nail something firm. "Agreed." They had enough food for a week. Their bus passes lasted another week. In seven days they would sail off the edge of the flat world.

Greta pulled out her English textbook at the table. Exams would give her something to focus on other than their slow drift toward doom. Ash was right—she shouldn't give up on it.

Ash reassembled the contents of their cupboards. When he had put everything back in its place, he rustled through the pantry. "Do we have any chocolate chips?" Patty had bought a few baking supplies for some Pinterest inspiration she'd had over Christmas, which had never gone anywhere. That app was like crack for her.

"No, I think Patty ate them all." Actually, Greta had finished the bag herself. "There's peanut butter. Maybe raisins."

Ash moved like a pro, pulling out a bowl, the measuring spoons, a recipe book. Greta watched him over the top of her English text. She stopped pretending to read as he leveled a cup of flour using the back of a butter knife, his eyebrows pinched in concentration. He scooped the last of their margarine into the bowl. A sweet sting, seeing him in the kitchen again, but by himself. He free-poured the vanilla. Their mom had always done that too.

Greta knew she should get up and offer to help, try to fill that empty space at his side. Somehow it felt disrespectful. Ash didn't ask her to either. Maybe he had avoided the kitchen to spare them both.

"Aren't you going to sneak some cookie dough?" Ash asked.

She smiled and took a pinch with her fingers, ducking her head away from him. The smell from the oven made the basement feel warmer. When the stove timer rang, Ash dropped a crumbly peanut-butter cookie by her elbow and loaded the rest on a paper plate.

"Raisins in cookies are evil," he said.

As Ash slipped on his shoes—no jacket—Greta followed behind him. "I'll go with you."

He nodded and led the way across the street and up Nate's steps. He rang the doorbell. Nate answered the door this time, opening it a crack. "Oh, hi." His red hair stood in tufts.

Ash swallowed and pushed the plate of cookies forward, like they would speak for him. Nate eyed the cookies, then Greta and Ash. So he wasn't going to make this easy. Standing behind Ash, Greta nudged his elbow.

"We—I—just wanted to say sorry for"—he cleared his throat—"you know, driving your car all crazy and..." He didn't finish the sentence.

Nate let the door fall open a little wider.

"I made you cookies," Ash said. "I hope you're not allergic to peanuts."

Nate took the plate but didn't say if he was allergic or not. He set them on a shelf of shoes beneath the coats. "You know," Nate said, crossing his arms over his chest, "I always wanted to meet you guys. Then when I did, I wasn't so sure anymore."

Greta felt guilty when he said it, even though she wasn't the one who'd nearly killed them all. Maybe for asking him to get involved in the first place? He'd spent the whole day driving them to Whitecourt and back, put up with their meltdowns and barely broke even for gas. He'd definitely gotten the worse end of the deal. Ash dropped his head too.

"It was kind of you to help us. We won't forget it," Greta said, turning and heading back down the steps.

"Yeah, thanks." Ash followed behind her.

They had both reached the path before Nate called out, "Do you want to come in? I'm making beef stew."

Ash and Greta looked at each other and then nodded. They sat at Nate's kitchen table while he chopped carrots and onions. His dad came home from work and gave them a smile that twitched on and off like a tic. "I hope everything, uh, went well," he said, clearing his throat. "It's good to be proactive with...those kinds of things." While Ash turned purple again, Greta pushed through the dirty feeling tugging her down and talked to Nate's dad about school and exams and the price of his winter gas bill—everything except their absentee parents.

. . . .

On Wednesday Greta came home from her English final to find Ash in a kitchen chair and Nate standing behind him with clippers. Ash's long brown wisps had fallen in a mesh of hair on the pocked hardwood.

"What are you guys doing?" she asked, peering over Ash's scalp.

Ash turned proudly in each direction so she could inspect it. Nate had shaved along the sides and back, leaving a longer section down the center.

"What'd you do that for?"

"All the cool kids are doing it," Ash said.

"Shut up." Greta flicked the back of his head.

Nate turned on the clippers and touched up an uneven spot.

"Don't you think it might hurt your chances of getting a job?" she asked.

"I'm pretty sure it won't hamper my ability to lower fries into a deep fryer."

"Touché."

Ash had applied for three jobs already that week, at two fast-food places and a snow-removal company. Nothing yet. Greta had applied as a cashier at the only supermarket in busing distance and at a place that made cinnamon buns in the mall. The bun place had told her she was underqualified. To bake pre-made cinnamon buns and make basic change. In the post-Christmas retail slump, few Help Wanted signs hung in store windows.

Now that she and Ash had no money, everything was about money. Greta had rationed their last few tomatoes, only to find one spotted with gray mold. She'd waited too long. She felt sick, dropping it in the garbage can.

Then a woman came to their door looking for donations for after-school programs for inner-city kids. She told Greta everything a thirty-dollar monthly donation would provide, and then talked the sum down as Greta politely declined each time. Finally the woman asked, "What about a one-time twenty-dollar donation?"

"I'm really sorry," Greta had said, "but I can't right now."

The woman left, looking at Greta like she was single-handedly responsible for child poverty.

The school had handed out sheets outlining fees for the second term, mostly for textbook rentals. Greta would take math, social studies and French. She had been enrolled in food studies too but had dropped it. It was unlikely any of *them* would take that class, but dropping it meant a spare at the end of the day. Quick exit. Three possible classes with Dylan, Rachel or Matt. A roulette wheel spun in her head, a ricocheting ball deciding her fate.

SIX

Thursday, no news about jobs or their dad. They took a bus to their aunt Lori's house and peered in her dark windows, then wedged a note under her door, asking her to call them the second she got back. Friday, Greta's and Ash's last exams, and a message on their answering machine from one of the fast-food places, requesting an interview with Ash. Ash actually smiled. Greta even saw a few teeth.

Saturday—the first day of February.

"Rent is due today," Ash said, pulling a bowl of instant oatmeal out of the microwave, "but I don't even have that interview until tomorrow afternoon."

"So we lay low, don't answer the door. Come and go when it's dark."

"Have you ever seen this guy?" Ash asked.

"No. Patty said he's old. Never goes out. Maybe he'll forget about rent."

"I don't know. She didn't say he was senile." Ash sat across from her at the table. "What about food?" They had enough for another three days, tops.

"We'll dip into our stash and go shopping today. Buy nothing that costs more than a dollar."

Ash nodded, stabbing at his oats. "Maybe Nate and his dad would help us?" He dropped his spoon in the bowl. That conversation would be painful.

"I don't know," Greta said. "It doesn't seem like they have a lot of money." Something about Nate's generic clothes and the worn furniture in their place reminded her of their own. His dad's pickup was more rust than truck around the wheel wells. "And we'd have to come clean to his dad." She didn't want to tell Ash she'd already texted Roger: **We're running out of food.** Ash wouldn't want to know about it, either the plea for help or the silence that followed.

"I'll go back to the mall today," she offered, "to see if anyone else is hiring. And we can bus to the library tomorrow and use their computers to check the online classifieds."

Ash nodded but looked away, his food untouched. They both saw it now, the bow of their ship tipping over the edge of the world.

"Eat it." She nudged his arm and looked down at the oatmeal. There were only two more packets in the box. They couldn't waste it.

They went to the mall first, and Greta filled out an application at a sub-sandwich place in the food court. As she walked past another counter, her stomach dropped.

Two drink dispensers stood side by side—one churning a peach-colored drink, and the other a deep purple. She stopped to watch the burbling purple juice, instantly nauseated. She swallowed against the saliva pooling at the back of her throat. Ash stopped beside her.

"What? You're thirsty?"

Greta shook her head and started walking again, still dogged by that sick feeling. And not just queasy—something else was mixed in there. Embarrassment tinged with…something. Like everyone around her could see she was less. Dirty. It was true she had embarrassed herself. It wasn't until she and Ash headed toward the mall exit that Greta could put a name to it. Near the entrance of a store selling chocolate, a mother tugged at the arm of a boy throwing a tantrum. She pulled a chocolate bar from his hand and dropped it back on the shelf while he whined and stomped his feet. People stared as they passed by. "You should be ashamed of yourself," the mother hissed, her cheeks red as she dragged the boy from the store.

You should be ashamed of yourself. Yes. Greta turned the phrase over in her mind, as though the words had been spoken just for her. She knew the feeling from before. Patty always had a way of making her feel small, like nothing. But it came more often now. Greta thought of how she'd shrunk from the couple making out on the bus. She'd even made Ash walk the long way to the mall exit, to avoid the posters hanging in the lingerie-store window.

She was quiet on the bus to the grocery store, where she trailed after Ash. They hit a sale on sixty-nine-cent canned soup ("MSG delight," Ash called it), and also bought a bag of apples and no-name mac and cheese.

Back at home, Ash wrestled with the key while holding the bag of apples. It stuck in the lock, the door falling wide open as he jerked his hand away. A handwritten note clung to the bottom of the door, dragging in an arc. Greta crouched to grab it, for one second believing it was some secret communication from Roger.

"*I haven't received a check for February's rent,*" Greta read. "*Please drop it in the mailbox at your earliest convenience. Elgin Doyle.*" Money, again. Always some reminder to nail them right back in reality.

"So much for the senile old man forgetting to charge us rent," Ash said, lifting the note from Greta's hand. "What kind of name is Elgin? How do even you pronounce that?"

Greta shrugged, wilting. "We'll have to talk to him."

"And tell him what?"

"The truth!" She pushed past him and dropped the grocery bags on the table. "We haven't done anything wrong, so why are we the ones sneaking around?"

Ash nodded, setting down the apples and the bag of canned soup.

"We tell him the truth, and what happens, happens," Greta said.

"Okay."

Greta lay in bed that night rehearsing the conversation, choosing her words. Ash had a job interview lined up. Maybe they could ask for more time. She dreaded it but also felt a tiny bud of relief. Their dad had left. They hadn't wanted him to, but he had. So if that meant Elgin Doyle kicked them out, or phoned the police or social services or whatever people did when parents left, that's what would happen.

Ash found her scrubbing refrigerator shelves the next morning.

"What are you doing?" he asked. "I thought we were going to the library today."

"No. We need to talk to Elgin and get that over with. I just didn't want to go too early and wake him up."

"Old people always get up early, Greta."

"I don't know about this one. The only time I hear him is during the night."

Ash watched her for a minute before lighting the oven. Then he pulled out the crisper drawers and rinsed them in the kitchen sink. Condiments—the only color in the stark fridge.

They waited until noon to climb the staircase between the two suites and knock on the door to Elgin's suite. Greta positioned herself slightly in front of Ash, prepared to do the talking. They knocked again. No answer.

"Maybe he's still sleeping," Greta said.

"How do we know when this man sleeps? Let's try the doorbell."

They walked around to the front of the house and rang the doorbell. As Greta raised her hand to ring it again, the floor behind the door creaked. She cleared her throat and clasped her hands in front of her.

The door opened an inch and stayed there. Greta squinted and leaned forward. She could make out the shape of an eye.

"Uh, hi, El—Mr. Doyle. We're your tenants from downstairs," Greta said, pretending she wasn't talking to a nearly closed door. "I'm Greta, and this is my brother, Ash."

The door swung open. "Oh, hello there."

Greta's mouth opened and closed. An elfin face, with thinning gray hair swept upward, like he'd slept on it wrong. His arms hung from a sleeveless undershirt, his bowed legs lost in a pair of fluorescent orange shorts—the kind runners wore in the eighties—that puffed out around his nearly hairless thighs. Black dress socks were pulled halfway up his calves, and the look was completed by a pair of sturdy leather oxfords.

Gone, whatever words she had rehearsed. They regarded each other.

"Mr. Doyle." Ash stepped forward. "Can we talk to you about February's rent?"

"Certainly. Come inside, please." Elgin stepped back from the door and motioned them forward.

Greta didn't move. Ash poked her in the back, nudging her on. She could feel him beside her, so she stepped into the entryway. Then she forgot about Elgin's lack of clothing. Warm, humid air, like being dropped in the middle of the Amazon. Green leaves bursting from everywhere. All signs pointed to a hydroponic pot-growing operation, but all Greta could see were ferns, spider plants and the round, stumpy leaves of rubber plants. Foliage covered the surface of every ledge, shelf and tabletop. Elgin motioned to the living room, toward a flowered couch and two recliners. "Have a seat. I was expecting…that woman."

So he, too, had been terrorized by Patty.

"Sorry if we interrupted you"—*while getting dressed*, Greta silently added. "We don't mind waiting." They settled side by side on the couch.

"No, no." Elgin perched on a nearby recliner. "You haven't interrupted anything."

Even more disconcerting. "Mr. Doyle—" she began.

"Elgin, please." He said it with a hard *g*. Mystery solved.

Greta wanted to unzip her sweater, but she wore only a tank top underneath, and she didn't want to show that much skin in front of him. Especially with him being so bare. She started to sweat, struggling to extract enough oxygen from the moist air.

"Warm, isn't it?" Elgin said. "If I set the thermostat to a regular temperature upstairs, I'm told it's cold in the basement. I don't want my tenants to suffer."

Greta didn't have the heart to tell him the basement felt like a refrigerator anyway, despite the sauna upstairs.

"It gets uncomfortable for me too," Elgin continued, glancing down at his bare arms and legs, "which is why I dress light. You don't mind, do you?"

Greta and Ash shook their heads in unison.

"Your feet don't get too warm in those shoes?" Greta asked. Or too heavy for his skinny legs to haul around?

"This pair has my best orthotics," Elgin said, lifting a foot. "Helps my back."

Bizarre but logical, all of it. "Elgin"—Greta cleared her throat—"we don't have rent money to give you today."

His caterpillar eyebrows kinked in the middle, like his back had just gone out. "No?"

"You see, we're still in high school..." Greta began.

"And our dad and stepmom were paying the rent..." Ash sighed, having to acknowledge his dead-to-him father and never-existed stepmother.

"But they...left." Greta nodded firmly—nothing more to say.

They all sat in silence for a moment, looking at each other.

"They left?" Elgin asked. "And when will they be back?"

"We don't know if they're coming back. They...took off, left us." Ash spat out the last words.

Elgin's eyebrows stayed kinked. "Just abandoned you?"

Greta fought the urge to cry, hearing it stated so plainly. She nodded.

"Well." Elgin sat back in his chair and rubbed his sagging knees. "What are you going to do?" So much for the adult taking charge of the situation.

Greta found her voice, grateful he hadn't asked why they'd left. "We're applying for lots of jobs."

"I have an interview this afternoon," Ash added.

"So"—Greta said, glancing at Ash—"we're hoping you could give us a little more time to come up with rent for February."

"But you're still in school. How will you earn enough to support yourselves?"

Elgin had voiced what Greta already knew in her gut. It was impossible. The whole crazy plan. But what else?

"Our aunt will be coming back from Arizona near the end of March," Ash said, "and we know she'll help us. We already left a note under her door for her to call us ASAP."

They both slumped back on the sofa as Elgin looked them over, two kids dragged into the principal's office.

"Well"—Elgin finally nodded—"let me know when you have the rent then. I'll have to..." He trailed off, then muttered, "She might...."

Greta and Ash looked at each other and stood before Elgin could change his mind.

"Thank you. Thank you." They tripped over each other as they scrambled for the door. Outside, the air stung their skin, stabbed down their throats and into their lungs. Greta looked at Ash's flushed face and laughed. He shook his head.

. . . . .

Later that afternoon, Greta met Ash at the door as he left to catch the bus to his job interview.

"Go get 'em, Tiger," she said.

Ash shot her a look.

"Remember, they'll probably ask you why you want to work at Freddy's Fries," she said. "Think of something good, like you really like helping people."

"Stop. Please. It hurts."

After an hour and a half, Greta heard the door swish open, the only sound in the quiet basement. "Hey." She set down the stack of old newspapers she'd been sorting in the living room.

"Hey."

"How'd it go?" So casual.

"I think it went okay." Ash took off his coat and headed for the bathroom.

"What kinds of things did they ask you?"

"You know, previous job experience, what's the most important part of customer service. Stuff like that."

Greta inwardly cringed. "And what did you say?"

"I'd rather not repeat the whole interview. I did my best."

Greta went to bed early that night to think. Waiting. Always waiting for results. Waiting to hear about the job. Waiting to hear from their dad. Waiting for Aunt Lori to get back from Arizona. Waiting to see who would be in her classes the next day—the first day of the new term. Her stomach twisted thinking about that, without the made-up daytime chores to distract her. A sick feeling trickled from her chest downward. She'd used up whatever got her through the last part of the previous term—hiding, skipping classes, faking every communicable virus known to humans—and crossed the finish line on fumes.

It was a far cry from November, after she'd been Sporty Spice and floated around on a cloud with Rachel and her friends. Greta remembered how, after Priya's party, Rachel had leaned in close at her locker and said, "So Dylan's been asking about the girl who was Sporty Spice."

"What about his girlfriend, the redhead?"

"Angela? That's over. You interested?"

Was that even a question? "Maybe." She'd tried out one of Rachel's coy looks.

"You should come to his basketball games. Matt plays on the team too."

"When's the next one?"

"Tomorrow night. I'll pick you up."

So she had sat with Rachel in the bleachers, red marks on her arm from Rachel squeezing it when the score was close. Watching how great Dylan's biceps looked in his basketball jersey, feeling a burst of something every time someone called his name. Rachel drove Greta home afterward, with Matt in the front and Dylan in the back seat next to her. He did an impression of their coach that made her laugh. They swapped stories about their stepparents. Dylan's stepdad wore a pair of socks at least three times before throwing them in the laundry. Greta told him about Patty's toilet-paper rationing.

On the drive home after the second game, Dylan had stretched one arm behind her and slid his other hand onto her knee. The only light glowed from the dash. In the front, Rachel and Matt skipped between radio stations. Dylan leaned in and kissed her on the cheek but didn't pull away again. He kissed her mouth, his arms, his body, around her. When they'd stopped in front of her house, he'd said, "Matt got the key to his parents' cabin at Pigeon Lake. Want to come to a party on Saturday night?" She'd said yes before he'd even finished the sentence.

Now, just a few months later, Greta felt unbearable panic at the thought of having to see Dylan, Matt or Rachel every day. In a hallway she could duck away with the crowd, or in the bathroom, wait it out in a stall. But in class every day? Walking in front of them. Feeling their eyes on her back. Noticing how they intentionally ignored her. Partner work. Group work. No. If finishing high school meant going through that every single day, she'd leave. It was a small price.

Greta wrapped the blanket tighter, rolled away from the steady window draft and waited for morning.

SEVEN

"It's minus thirty-eight degrees today, with wind chill," Ash told Greta as she stumbled into the kitchen. Even with the oven blazing, she felt the invasion of a hundred tiny currents seeping through the cracks of the basement suite.

Every current stood in solidarity with her, protesting the start of the new term. She'd radiated misery, and winter had joined her. *I'm here*. It pressed in on the house and prickled the air. Air this cold sought vengeance.

Greta eyed Ash as they stood in the entryway, preparing to catch the bus. She wound a black woolen scarf around her neck, up over her mouth, until it touched her nose. Then she zipped up her parka and pulled the hood over her head, leaving a narrow slit for her eyes. For one second, she thought how this would impress Roger—always on her about dressing for the weather—and then scoffed at herself. Roger didn't even care that they were running out of food. The right choice of outerwear didn't matter now.

Ash zipped up his coat and stuffed his hands in his pockets.

"Bundle up, Ash." She sounded like Roger. "It's minus thirty-eight. Put something on your head. You'll need gloves too."

He shrugged. "I'll be fine."

"You cannot will your skin not to freeze and fall off. Here." She dug through a box of mittens, scarves, tuques. "Here's Dad's hat. Put it on."

"But it's got a pom-pom."

"So? Take it off before you go inside."

Ash headed for the door. "No, thanks."

"Fine. Freeze." She followed a step behind, choking back more words.

The air stung the skin around her eyes and singed her nostrils. Ash grimaced too and quickened his pace. Down the path and onto the sidewalk. Past one house, two houses. Greta heard his sharp intake of breath and looked over to see him pressing his bare hands against his ears. Half a block down, he stuffed one hand back into his coat pocket and held the other against his forehead, his face pained. The woolen fibers of her scarf frosted white from her breath and stuck to her nose. Through her gloves, her fingertips numbed. By the end of the block, Greta struggled to blink, her eyelashes starting to freeze together. Ash's face looked gaunt and white—a sun-bleached skeleton. His ears glowed tomato red, standing out from his newly shorn scalp. The cold burned.

She stopped abruptly at the end of the street, the thought coming before the words formed.

"What?" Ash asked, his mouth stiff and tight.

"Our bus passes expired on Friday—the end of January. We can't take the bus."

They stood in silence, each one following that thought to a dead end. They didn't have money to replace both passes. Only one. And even one would take all their money. No way they could walk to school—not even with all the pom-pom tuques in the world. The air pierced their skin through their jeans, numbing their thighs.

"Let's go back," Greta said.

"I can't feel any part of me." Ash nodded and strode back toward their house. Greta jogged to keep up. Then Ash started to jog, and she fell farther behind, each step shooting sparks through her numb toes. Her boots seemed made of paper.

Inside the basement, Ash fell against the closed door and gasped, suffocated by the cold. He blew on his fingers and pressed his palms to his ears.

Greta flopped on the couch, thick in her winter gear, before bolting up again. "What about Nate? We could ask him for a ride."

Ash's eyes flickered toward Nate's house and the evil outdoors. "Yeah. Okay. Just a sec."

"I'll go catch him." Greta charged up the steps and found Nate in his driveway, attempting to start his yellow Volvo.

The car made a thick *chug* sound before dying. Then again. The third time, something caught and the motor turned over—clunky, painful. Nate unplugged the engine block heater from an extension cord trailing from the garage. He spotted Greta. "Rebus doesn't like the cold," he said, blowing out a cloud of frosty air. He wore an orange tuque with a black pom-pom, tufts of hair jutting out from beneath it. Greta noticed ice crystals forming on his eyebrows.

"Can we get a ride?" she asked. "Our bus passes expired, and we don't have the money to buy more." After what he'd seen of their family, she was sure he could handle this level of honesty.

"No problem. I wondered why you didn't ask sooner."

She sat in the front, and Ash hunkered in the back. Nate reached past the steering wheel and turned up the heat. But Rebus didn't really have heat. Not truly. More like blowing around air a degree or two warmer than outdoors. Even so, Ash's face was a nearly human color by the time they got to school.

In the school parking lot they wove a path to the door, stepping in snowy grooves flattened by tires and footsteps. They each meandered on their own path. Greta watched the back of Nate's head, how he didn't pull the tuque off before walking through the back entrance.

"Nate!" she called.

He turned and waited for her, trailing behind him in the busy hallway. "If you're not doing anything at lunch, why don't you sit with us?"

He smiled, his teeth even whiter than his pale skin. "Okay. I'll find you in the cafeteria."

"Check the dark corners."

He laughed and walked away. And then it was real. Every minute another step up a bald cliff face. By the end of the day, she would either fall to her death or triumph at the top. "Ash." She grabbed his arm as he started past her. "Let me see your schedule."

He pulled it, crumpled, out of a binder and showed her.

"You're in math this term too," she said. "If I need you to, will you drop your class and take it with me? I'll know whether I need you to after today."

Ash frowned. "I was hoping to take art during that block."

"Please, Ash. I'm asking nicely." *I'm begging.*

Her fingers pinched his arm. Ash looked down at them and then back to her face. "Why do I have to take math with you?"

Tell him. "Just say yes. Please." She could do it with him sitting beside her.

"Okay." He waited for Greta to drop her hand before stepping back. "See you at lunch." She watched him walk away still rubbing his arm.

You can do this. Terror plus nausea. Nauseous terror. It swirled through her, a noxious gas, as she walked to social studies. Three classes. Just three classes to get through.

At the door of the classroom, she paused and surveyed it, front to back. A few familiar faces from her other classes but not Dylan, Rachel or Matt. She chose a desk near the back, where she could see everyone coming through the door. The teacher, who looked younger than Greta, rifled through a stack of papers at the front, obviously stressed. Greta watched the clock, waiting for the class to begin so she would know for sure.

Two minutes left. Her shoulders began to unclench. One class safe? Then Angus—one of the guys from the cabin party—paused in the doorway and checked the room over like she had. Greta held her breath, watching for who would follow him. No. Just him. He picked a desk not far from hers—one of the only ones left—and tossed her a cold look over his shoulder. Greta pretended not to notice.

The second Angus sat down, the smell of his cologne or body spray hit her and, in the next beat, a wall of nausea. That cheap woodsy scent…something about that night. Sweat. Hands on her body, breath by her ear. Bile moved up her throat, burning. Greta lurched from her desk, scooping her books in her arms as she fled. The teacher paused, and heads swiveled in her direction. Greta burst into the empty hall and stumbled to the bathroom, locking herself in a stall. *What's wrong with me?* She took deep breaths and swallowed, her heart slowing now. She couldn't assign the feeling to one thing, but that cologne formed a part of the fog of that night at the cabin, tied in with the blur of bodies, the nausea of the purple drink, memories like gray forms—almost there. *Pull yourself together.* She took a long drink from the water fountain until her stomach stopped convulsing, but couldn't bring herself to go back inside the classroom.

Greta left for her French class early, creeping through the silent hall, and sat outside the door until the bell rang.

Even though she'd moved at the pace of a turtle, her breath came short and shallow. At the door she paused and looked the room over. Sam—Baby Spice—sat near the front. Greta's eyes whipped through every row, checking for the others. No one she recognized. Her chest loosened.

Then Sam turned in Greta's direction, giving her a tight smile before snapping to face forward again. *Et tu, Sam? Et tu?* That definitely wasn't an invitation to sit in the empty desk beside her. So much for being the nice one.

At lunchtime Greta crouched low in the cafeteria, hunched in her and Ash's usual corner, behind a ficus tree. Greta had suspected it before—but had never fully realized till now—that the table with Dylan, Matt, Rachel, Priya, Sam and all their hangers-on was the hub of the whole cafeteria. Really, the whole school. She'd been there, sitting *right* there, and now she had to crouch behind a ficus tree to eat her microwaved Mr. Noodles. Everything gift wrapped for her—"on a silver platter," as Patty would say—and she'd still messed it up. Why had she ever gone to the cabin?

Rachel had driven her there, nearly an hour outside the city, with the windshield wipers beating against the steady fall of fat November snowflakes. A layer of white coated a line of empty cabins nicer than anything Greta had ever lived in. Rachel pulled in behind Matt's dad's SUV, beside a small A-frame cabin.

Dylan had swung the door open and leaned against the doorjamb. He wore a loose plaid shirt over a white T-shirt, baggy jeans. It was obvious he'd already had a couple.

The grin gave him away, like Rachel's car was delivering a winning lotto ticket. And he had that amused look —just waiting for someone to make him laugh. His loose brown curls slightly disheveled. Greta had wanted to touch him.

Matt came and stood behind him, a beer in one hand. "Heeeeeyyy!" he and Dylan called to Rachel and Greta at the same time.

Rachel laughed. "Those two."

Inside the cabin, she hovered behind Rachel as Matt and Dylan set up beer pong and mixed some purple punch that made her eyes water from three feet away. How could she keep up with them? They obviously did this every weekend.

Priya—all legs in a little dress and tall boots—and Sam arrived shortly after. Rachel pulled Greta into the living-room area, where two tiny loveseats and a wicker chair bumped each other. A burning log in the fireplace radiated the only heat. "You should probably know," Rachel whispered, "that Dylan used to date…"

Don't say Priya, Greta had thought. Priya already seemed to own every room she entered—a goddess ready to shower commoners with blessings or wrath.

"…Priya last year," Rachel finished. "I'd keep one eye on her, if I were you."

More people crowded into the kitchen and living room, and they started a game of beer pong. Greta tried not to gag on the yeasty, lukewarm beer. For a few minutes, nothing, then the buzz hit her head, her legs a little off balance.

She leaned back on Dylan's chest, his chin resting against her hair. She stayed close to him, watching Priya work her way around the room as more people arrived.

As the noise climbed around them, Dylan poured two cups of his homemade punch and led Greta, bumping shoulders and stepping on feet, across the living room. He dropped into the wicker chair and pulled her into his lap. She fit there, in the curve of his body. Tucking her legs up, she lay against his chest. He ran his fingers up under the cuff of her jeans, against her bare skin. She knew there was a reason she'd shaved her legs.

"You're the most beautiful girl here," he said, his mouth by her ear. She lay still, his heartbeat making her sleepy.

After a sip of punch, which burned going down, she tried to put it on the floor. "I think I'm good for now," she said. "I might be designated driver."

Dylan laughed. "I don't think you'll be driving anytime soon. Don't die on me now, Greta."

She'd drained the cup. After Dylan went for a refill, things got blurry. Memories smeared or chopped in pieces. Rachel sitting close to Matt on one of the sofas. Priya and Sam dancing to a song playing on Priya's phone. Some guy with a goatee smoking nearby, tapping ashes into an empty bottle. On a trip to the bathroom, Angus stepping close to her, smiling, his hand on her waist. Talking close to her ear. Her reaching to touch his dreads, but Dylan appearing, pulling her away. Doing a shot with Sam. Matt and Dylan streaking out the front door, shirtless, into the snow. Dylan kissing her in the kitchen, tasting like fruit punch. Angus's face a storm cloud over Dylan's shoulder.

Her last memory of that night was of being stretched out on her belly on the leather sofa, Priya by her head, bent over to talk to her. "Are you okay?" Her hand on Greta's shoulder. "Do you want me to take you home?" Through an eye slit, Greta had seen Priya's jacket and the tops of her long black boots, the keys in her hand. Greta had tried to tell her to go away, to stay away from Dylan, but the words wouldn't come. She'd turned her head away from Priya.

Now, in the cafeteria, Greta turned away from Priya again, just as Ash and Nate appeared. Nate sat between them on the bench, leaning forward with the same expression as a dog with its head out the window. He immediately launched into a game of Would You Rather.

"Would you rather"—he twisted his mouth—"eat an entire pig or wear a wig for the rest of your life?"

Ash's brow furrowed. Greta stepped into her role as the-one-who-is-patient-with-weird things. "I'd probably rather eat a pig." Wigs were itchy, sweaty.

"The *whole* pig, raw. Every part. Just sit down and eat a raw pig."

She grimaced. "Okay, maybe not. I'd wear the wig then."

"That's every day," Nate said. "Night and day, from now until you die."

"Uh, I don't know." She honestly didn't know. Through the ficus leaves, she saw Chloe—Ginger Spice— slip her arm around Dylan's waist and hang her thumb from his back pocket.

Not surprising. Greta had noticed her always hovering around Dylan. That was the thing about having a lineup of people wanting to date the same guy. Always someone ready to step over your corpse and take your place. Just as she had done with Priya and Angela.

One more class to survive. Math.

Greta arrived before the teacher and found the door locked. A middle-aged black woman came up behind her, picking a key from a lanyard. "You're keen, aren't you?" The teacher winked and swung the door open for Greta. "I'm Mrs. Flynn. You here for math?"

Greta just nodded—no energy for small talk. She found the perfect desk in the back corner and waited for the room to fill. A minute later more people wandered in, dropping books on desks, their heads turned to one another. Some girl from Greta's bio class last term. A guy from her French class. Strangers. Strangers. A bunch of people on their phones. Greta saw the long black hair first and felt her heart pound her chest. No—a different head of long black hair.

Mrs. Flynn called in a straggler from the hallway and shut the door. She started talking about class rules and expectations as she made her way to the front of the room. Greta didn't hear another word. All three classes free of Dylan, Rachel and Matt. Angus and Sam she could handle. She closed her eyes and felt the lead escape her bones, float to nowhere. She hadn't even known it was there. Her chest expanded wide—more air than she thought possible—for the first time all day. No, for the first time in nearly three months.

She could do it. They could do it. All of it. Come to school. Graduate. Get jobs and move past this. Everything was possible. She closed her eyes and felt her body float from her desk—so light.

. . . .

After Nate dropped them off at home, Greta said, "Ash, you don't have to transfer to my math class." She faced forward to hide her smile.

"Why not?"

"I have a good teacher. Take art instead."

"You were always better at it than me anyway. I don't think I would have been much help to you."

She unlocked the door, Ash nearly stepping on her to escape a gust of wind. He beat her to the oven in the kitchen. "I'm thinking of moving the couch," he said, pointing to the middle of the kitchen floor. "To right here."

Greta smiled, then noticed the light blinking on the answering machine. *Dad.* Always her first impulse, no matter how hard she tried to stamp it out. She pressed *Play* as Ash reached for the matchbox.

"Hi there, Ash. This is Ed, the manager of Freddy's Fries." His voice sounded tinny through the answering machine. Both Ash and Greta froze and watched the machine as though Ed himself stood there.

"Thank you for your interview yesterday. I wanted to let you know that we've gone with another candidate

at this time." He cleared his throat. "Have a good day."
Click.

She searched for something hopeful, supportive, to say.
Something to say it was okay. The *have a good day* a final
kick in the crotch. She had nothing.

Ash looked at her. "Tomato or chicken noodle?" he asked.

"We had tomato yesterday. Chicken noodle." She didn't
want oversalted canned soup though. She wanted a steak,
medium rare, and a baked potato with bacon bits and sour
cream. She wanted a salad full of green things not found in
her fridge, with a dressing not from a Kraft bottle. Cheesecake
with melted chocolate sauce, the kind that felt heavy in her
belly and that she would regret just a little.

And she wanted to disappear into her room so she didn't
have to try. Let herself plummet over the edge of the world.
But it wouldn't be fair to Ash, leaving him to plummet alone.
"Want to watch *Quiz Kings*?" she asked. It was a trivia show
for old people that Patty had got them all hooked on, and it
seemed to run about five times a day.

They sat on the couch with their knees pulled up, slouching
toward the middle, where the broken springs sagged. Greta
turned on the TV, right in the middle of a commercial for
men's underwear, all abs and bulges. She closed her eyes
and counted to twenty, trying to stave off the feeling of dirty
panic. She couldn't handle it—not right now. *Ash is here. I'm
okay. Ash is here. I'm okay.* Ash got up to relight the oven,
taking the edge off the room, and brought in mugs of soup.
The next commercial came on, this one for breakfast cereal.

Greta focused on its annoying jingle and how the mug burned against her palms.

"Maybe you were right about the haircut," Ash finally said, settling next to her again. More likely it was Ash's *give-me-a-job-or-die* persona. *You want Coke with that? Want me to shove your face in the deep fryer?*

"No," Greta said. "It wasn't the haircut. Don't worry— you'll find something better. I will too."

A knock on the door between their suite and Elgin's. Greta pointed to the oven. Ash scrambled to turn it off as Greta eased the door open. There Elgin was, in the same undershirt and fluorescent running shorts as before. Greta didn't want to talk about jobs, bills or rent right then. Just *Quiz Kings* and toxic soup.

Elgin clasped his hands in front of him—a formal gesture for someone standing in that outfit. "Just wondering if you kids had heard about that job yet," he said.

Greta waved him inside. "Uh, that one didn't work out," she said. "We'll keep trying."

Elgin's wild-man eyebrows shot up, then dropped low. "That right? Okay, keep me—" He stopped and looked around. Greta noticed the dust on the TV stand and the pile of blankets by the couch. "Sure is chilly down here. Is it always like this?" He seemed to shrink, his clothes hanging looser on his frame.

Usually colder. They'd had the oven on for a few minutes. They nodded. But how could they complain, living there for free at this point? Elgin walked farther into the living room, then into the kitchen, his hands out to test the air. "It's a little warmer in the kitchen."

"We were"—Ash cleared his throat—"cooking something."

"And the bedrooms?" Elgin asked.

"Colder," Greta said.

Elgin eyed the kitchen counter with the empty soup can, a ring of fluorescent yellow goo dribbling off the lid. "Do you have enough food?"

Greta shrugged. "We have a little."

Elgin crossed his arms against the cold, his face settling in a grimace. "I may have a space heater upstairs." He climbed the staircase between the suites, leaving the top door open behind him. Ash raised an eyebrow at Greta, and they both waited.

No one moved until he came back down again, his arms empty. "I must've loaned it to my daughter."

"That's okay," Greta said, starting to turn away.

"But…" Elgin clasped his hands again. "Um…"

Greta and Ash faced him. His eyebrows worked overtime.

"If you like"—Elgin coughed—"I have a spare room upstairs."

Greta leaned forward slightly, her mouth opening. Ash frowned and flipped his hair from his eyes.

"You could stay there for now," Elgin continued, "until your aunt comes back." His words came fast and clear now. "It's warm. I have money for food, but I hate grocery shopping. I've been having groceries delivered and paying someone to shovel the walk too. I don't like going outside much in winter. Maybe you could take on those things and help around the house in exchange for room and board?"

Greta's eyes darted to Ash, reading his thoughts. "If it's easier for you, Mr. Doyle, Elgin"—she paused—"we could work for you and still stay in the basement. We're kind of used to the cold now, and we don't want to, uh, disturb you."

"That's very thoughtful," Elgin said, "but I may have to move your belongings into the garage and rent out this space. You see, I have other…financial obligations."

Greta nodded, trying to digest what he'd said. Could they live with Elgin? All the plants? The lack of pants? They'd lived with Patty and survived. "Thanks so much for that. Can I just talk to my brother for a minute?"

Elgin nodded and left. Not like they had much choice. *No, Elgin, we prefer to keep living in your basement for free.*

The second they heard the upstairs door close, Ash turned to Greta. "I don't know, Greta. He's kind of weird."

"We're weird, Ash," she snapped. "Is anything about us or our lives normal?" When he didn't answer, she said, "He's just an old man. I'm pretty sure the two of us can take him if he tries anything."

"So we're going to live with our landlord," he said, his voice flat.

"I don't see that we exactly have a choice until we get jobs or Aunt Lori comes back. It's either Elgin or a tarp under a bridge."

Ash sighed and shook his head. "This just gets better and better."

"But Ash"—she grabbed his arm as he turned away—"don't leave me alone with him. Ever."

"Okay." He opened his mouth and closed it again, watching her face.

"I mean it." She didn't let go. "If I have to go to the bathroom, you're standing outside that door."

"You think—?" He started to say more but stopped himself. "Okay. I'll stay with you."

Greta gathered her stuff from the bathroom and emptied her drawers into a suitcase. Ash took even less time, clearing his things from a shelf in the storage room into a cardboard box with one swoop of his arm. He went upstairs first.

Greta stood at the base of the staircase, one hand on the doorknob and the other around her suitcase handle. She looked over the suite, wondering if there was anything else she needed or some keepsake she wanted with her. A bad taste settled in her throat. Everything bore the taint of Patty, from the faint scent of her cigarettes to the memory of her shouting at them for playing near her hideous porcelain-dog collection. A mark attached to everything

She'd told Ash the truth when she'd said it didn't shock her that Roger had left. Like how she knew, at least one time per winter, their car wasn't going to start. She didn't want it to happen, but it didn't surprise her. She gripped the doorknob tighter. But seven years. Seven years he'd made excuses for Patty's anger, tried to make them share the blame in her tornado of drama. They'd been kids—imperfect, noisy, messy. He'd played middle man between a wolf and two sheep, trying to justify why the wolf always tore at them. Trying to please that rabid wolf. And for a while they'd tried to please it, too, believing they couldn't do anything right and if only they'd try a little harder. Roger had failed them for seven years. That part, unforgivable. Leaving, just a technicality.

She slammed the door behind her, shaking the frame, and climbed the stairs without looking back.

EIGHT

When Greta reached the top of the stairs, Elgin pointed in the direction of his spare room. He really didn't need to—the layout of the upstairs mirrored the basement. It made sense that his bedroom was the larger one by the bathroom, and the spare room the replica of Greta's downstairs.

She found Ash sitting on the edge of a daybed with a pink-and-white bedspread, his box by his feet. Pale pink paint covered the walls, and a white dresser and a pile of stuffed animals sat in one corner. In contrast to all the pastels, a poster of the band Swamp Demons hung above the dresser, showing tattooed band members climbing out of some kind of cesspool.

"You're probably used to sharing a room," Elgin said, dragging in an inflated air mattress, "but there's only one real bed in here."

Sharing. Of course he wouldn't know about the storage closet. They hadn't shared a room since they were ten. "This is great," Greta said, sliding the mattress onto the floor. "We can bring blankets from downstairs."

"No need," Elgin said, opening the closet door and pointing to a stack of folded bedding. Greta broke out in a sweat just looking at it.

"You know, you can probably turn the heat down, now that no one's living downstairs," she said. "It might save you on your gas bill." Weren't seniors always concerned about utility bills?

"Better not," Elgin said, hauling out the thickest blanket and a few sheets and placing them on the air mattress. "I don't want those pipes to freeze. That'd be a real mess."

Greta smiled. "Thank you."

Elgin nodded and left. Ash made up the air-mattress bed, grabbed a pillow from the daybed and lay down.

Greta asked, "What are you doing?"

Ash looked up. "What?"

"You sleep in the bed. The real bed."

"That's okay. I'm used to it."

"Get up, Ash. You're sleeping in the bed."

"Whatever, Greta. It doesn't matter."

He hadn't even questioned it—that was the sad part.

"It's your turn." She kicked at his foot. "No more sleeping on the floor."

"Well, maybe we can alternate," Ash said.

"No. From now until we leave you're sleeping in the bed." She was as guilty as Patty and Roger of letting things slide. No more. "I'm not moving until you get up here."

"Okay. Fine." He held up his hands, resigned, and settled on the bed. But smiled.

In the night, lying on top of the blankets wearing only a T-shirt and shorts, she heard Elgin shuffle by the door. She sat up, suddenly wide awake, and lifted a hand to shake Ash, in case he entered their room. But his footsteps continued down the hallway. Greta listened for him for a long time but heard only the creaking and shifting of the house.

The next morning they tiptoed around, speaking in whispers. Elgin's door remained closed. Bright sun through the living-room window lit the whole upper floor. After drinking at least a liter of water, Greta stood in the middle of the living room, surrounded by sun and plants, and felt the warmth on her bare arms.

"Greta!" Ash hissed from the kitchen. "Did you see this?" He held up a package of bacon with a yellow sticky note on it. She came closer to read it: *This should be eaten soon.* Ash nearly giggled.

"Guess what I'm cooking while you're in the shower?" he said.

Sunshine. Green leaves. Bacon. Best morning ever.

At minus twenty degrees, the air shucked their skin after being in Elgin's semitropical suite. They jogged across the street to Nate's house and waited in the entryway while he rummaged for his keys.

Greta had mapped it out in her head, the hallways and routes that would get her to her classes with the least chance of running into Dylan, Rachel or Matt. In social studies, she sat as far as possible from Angus. No cologne today. Still, it was like her body remembered, and her mind lagged behind the teacher's words, hearing them but not comprehending. When it was time to work independently, Angus twisted in his desk, craning to see around the people between him and Greta.

"Greta," he shout-whispered. She looked down at her binder, pretending not to hear. Everyone around them turned to stare. "Greta, Arjun here's a basketball player."

Out of the corner of her eye, she saw Angus pointing to a tall, acne-pocked guy sitting beside him. She recognized him from Dylan's games. Arjun turned and checked her out. Greta's face burned.

"There's a closet back there." Angus motioned with his chin. Greta didn't turn to look. "You could...you know." In the aisle between him and Arjun, he made a jerk-off gesture with his hand. A few sniggers broke out around them. Greta couldn't speak or move, every vein in her body hardening.

"Shut up, Angus," Arjun said, turning back to the book on his desk. Everyone else shifted away too.

Greta knew she should feel better, the spotlight on her switched off. But it had felt, when Angus spoke, as if her clothes had been torn away in front of thirty sets of eyes. As though she really had followed Arjun to the closet, let him do whatever, with everyone laughing at her outside the door. *Nasty girl. Easy.* She dug her nails into her palms, not wanting Angus to see he'd gotten to her, choking, drowning in the purple-punch feeling.

In French class, she sat in absolute silence for most of the class, until a girl next to her asked to partner up to practice a conversation about ordering in a café. As Greta struggled to say the new words, she started to forget about Angus and Arjun. And the girl looked at her like she was a normal person, like her only concern was if Greta accidentally pronounced all the silent letters. By the end of class Greta was thinking of Nate and Ash, their corner in the cafeteria and the BLT sandwiches they had brought for lunch.

Then Priya appeared right outside the door of the French classroom, her books tucked under one arm. Greta nodded at her, dropped her head and attempted to duck by.

"Greta, wait!" Priya called, catching her by the arm.

"What?" Greta turned, her anger surprising her. She owed them nothing.

"I just want to talk to you for a sec." Priya tried to make eye contact with Greta, her face curious.

"My brother's waiting for me," Greta said, shaking off Priya's hand.

"Please. It won't take long." Greta had never heard her say *please* before.

"Fine, but right here." She wasn't going to be dragged into some kind of *Survivor* tribal council with the rest of them.

Priya pulled her to the side of the hallway as bodies pushed past on their way toward the cafeteria. Greta stared at her, challenging.

"Well"—Priya cleared her throat—"I noticed things have been a little tense between you and everyone else for a while now." By *everyone else* she meant her minuscule group of super-important friends, of course.

Greta raised her eyebrows but didn't speak. She didn't have to try with Priya anymore.

"Can I ask why?" Priya said. "What happened?"

"They didn't tell you?"

Priya shook her head. "Whenever I asked, everyone either shut down or got mad. So I stopped asking."

"Why do you care?"

Priya sighed. "Look, I know it's none of my business. About a year ago, Rachel screwed me over big-time. I know what they can be like. I kind of wondered if the same thing had happened to you."

Greta looked away from Priya. They probably just wanted to see what she would say behind their backs.

"And Dylan"—Priya paused—"I know him too." Greta snapped back to Priya's face. "We were together for a few weeks last year. Let's just say I wasn't willing to do certain things on, like, the first or second date." *Things you were willing to do. Slut.* "He didn't want to wait."

That shame—waiting in the wings since social studies—crept out of hiding and oozed through her body. She swallowed, her stomach queasy. Like on the morning at the cabin, after the party.

She'd woken to a wave of nausea rolling over her. Cold air pressed against her bare arm, left outside the blanket. She'd pulled it in, held it against her body. Her bare breast. Her eyes had jolted open, a shock ripping through her. She lay in a four-poster bed in a nearly empty loft. A flowered quilt covered her naked body. Around her, the room shone impossibly bright through a curtainless window. Not a single sound. Except breathing.

Greta had moved her eyes in its direction. Dylan's loose brown waves spread across the pillow, his head turned away from her. Bare shoulder and arm over the blanket. She lifted the blanket and glanced down at him. Bare back and ass. Another wave of nausea, so strong she sucked in air through clenched teeth. Maneuvering onto her back, she had tried to breathe slow and steady.

Her body hurt. Her left knee throbbed when she shifted. Some vague recollection of falling down and arms helping her up. She was sore. There. She reached her hand between her legs and drew her fingers to her face. Blood. She bolted upright, tearing back the quilt on her side. Bleeding on that bed would've been more humiliating than a public stoning. Her discarded clothes lay on the sheet, pressed flat by her body. Her wrinkled shirt had caught a few drops—the sheet beneath still white. She exhaled. She could wear her jacket to cover the shirt.

Dylan still slept. Some tiny relief in her rattled core. Someone, something, had smashed her insides. Every organ, every blood vessel, was still there, but fragmented and in the wrong spots. If only she could've been home, alone in her room, to piece it back together. She pulled on her jeans—underwear missing—then bra and wrinkled shirt. Her jacket hid the stain on the shoulder. She couldn't look at it. A second burst of relief, being covered by her own clothes again.

Then Greta lowered herself onto the bed, on top of the blankets, and stared at the ceiling. *Breathe in. Breathe out.* Her stomach twisted again, but less urgently. Dylan lifted his head off the pillow and looked around. He reached over and felt her beside him, then shifted to face her.

"Hey." He smiled. Still a beautiful smile. "Already dressed?"

Her head bypassed the shattered core. "I've been awake for a while."

"How are you feeling?"

She blew out a puff of air. "A little rough."

He laughed and pulled her closer. "You should have told me you were such a lightweight. I would have gone easy on you."

What did he mean by that? "Yeah, I don't drink a lot." *Go with that one.*

"And don't worry"—his voice dropped low, even though no one else was around—"I used a condom."

Her gut coiled in a tight ball. *Okay. Condom. Good. One less thing to worry about.* Teachers in health class had been pushing condoms since the seventh grade. Ninety-eight percent effective if used correctly. "Thanks." *Thanks?*

"No, thank you." He laughed again and rose from the bed. Greta looked away as he got dressed.

Taking her hand, Dylan led her down a ladderlike staircase to the living room. In the nearby kitchen, Matt tossed garbage into a bag and emptied half-filled cups down the sink. He didn't even look at her. Rachel stepped out of the bathroom, dressed in her clothes from the night before. Everyone else was gone.

"Should we start a fire?" Rachel asked. The cabin was only slightly warmer than outside.

"No." All eyes turned to Greta when she spoke. "We should go." How quickly could they get out of there? She'd feel better once they left. The nausea tumbled in her stomach like a wretched boulder, rolling around her shattered insides.

Before anyone could speak, Greta started gathering cups and empties from the living room. Her head went *clunk* every time she bent down, her legs off-kilter when she stood up again. She steadied herself, one hand on the sofa. Dylan came and stood behind her, wrapping his arms around her like he had the night before, making her stronger. She wished they could curl up in the wicker chair again, stop everything from swimming around her.

Too soon, he let go, ducking when Matt threw an empty soda bottle at him. "Didn't you get enough of that last night?" They wrestled in the kitchen.

Greta lowered herself onto the sofa and closed her eyes. She'd had sex with Dylan. She'd had sex, period.

As they left the cabin, Greta watched Matt slip the key under the welcome mat, the wooden slats beneath it untouched by snow. "In case we want to come back again," he said. "I don't want to sneak it out twice."

On the drive home, Matt and Dylan mostly talked basketball. The car felt stifling, heat blasting through every vent. Greta cracked her window open until everyone turned to look at her. They passed a car flipped in the ditch, its tires angled unnaturally toward the sky. A dead beetle. In the window reflection, Greta saw her black eyeliner smudged around her eyes. Face pale, her lipstick long rubbed away. She was a human train wreck, an embarrassment. Rachel couldn't get her home fast enough. A shower. Quiet. A place where she could close her door and pick through all the little shards.

Rachel dropped her off first, so Dylan and Matt saw her sad stucco house in the light of day. Another point in the humiliation category. She slipped out of the car before Dylan could kiss her, the taste in her mouth like compost. But a tiny relief when Rachel pulled away before she walked down the steps to the basement. Somehow going in that door seemed worse.

And another relief at finding Roger and Patty out grocery shopping.

"Are you okay?" Ash sat on the sofa, the TV on, and watched her walk past.

"I'm fine." She kept going.

Her dingy room with the unmade bed was the most beautiful sight in the universe. She lowered herself onto the edge of the mattress, her knee throbbing again. Ash knocked and let himself in, standing over her. Greta shrank from the box of onion crackers in his hand, the picture on the front making her want to heave again.

Ash smiled and waved it a little closer. "Not hungry?" He cocked his head and squinted. "Nice hickey, by the way. Don't be such a cliché, Greta."

"Shut up! Get out of here!" she shouted, making him step back.

"Fine." He threw up his hands and turned to leave.

He made it to the door before she said, "Actually, come back."

"What? Why?"

"Just get over here."

He came back and stood in the same place. "What?"

"Sit down."

He did. Greta shoved his body so he faced away from her on the bed. Then she leaned against his back. "Wait." She took off her jacket and dropped it to the floor. He wouldn't see the stain, facing the other way.

"Why am I—"

"Shut up, Ashwin."

They sat with their backs against each other, holding each other up. After a minute Greta let her head fall back, resting it against his neck. She felt his body heat escaping through his thin T-shirt. She swore she could feel his heartbeat. It tied in with the rise and fall of his chest. Maybe that was it, some throwback to their time in utero. Although it would freak him out for her to say it.

"Greta—"

"Shh."

Everything had slowed, finally calm. She'd wanted to say, *Don't tell Dad*, but somehow knew those words would hurt to say out loud. So she lowered herself to her pillow and slept.

. . . .

Outside the French classroom now, Priya squinted at her, leaning closer. "Did something happen with Dylan?"

No way she was talking about this with Priya.

"What did Rachel do to you?" Greta asked.

Priya hesitated and looked around for eavesdroppers. "Rachel wanted to be with Matt since forever, so she started a rumor about his then-girlfriend cheating on him. They were probably going to break up anyway, but that was the final straw. After Rachel and Matt got together, his ex confronted Rachel, in front of Matt, about making up this lie. Rachel blamed it on me. Matt said he didn't care, but there are hallways I still can't walk down without being afraid his ex or her friends will beat me up. So that's when I saw the real Rachel."

"Why didn't you warn me about her and Dylan?"

Priya looked annoyed. "And you would've believed me?"

Greta thought of Dylan at Priya's party, holding her strong when she stumbled, looking down on her like some knight in shining armor. Rachel's sweet smile versus Priya's resting-bitch face. She was right. "Probably not."

They regarded each other, unsure of where to go next.

"If what you're saying is true, why don't you find some new friends to hang out with?" Greta asked.

"Now? Half the school hates us, and the other half wants to *be* us. Who's going to accept a cast-off at this point? No"—she shook her head—"I just have to survive a few more months.

Then I'm going to university in Toronto, and I'll never have to deal with all *this* again." She waved her hand to encompass the whole school.

So Priya was doing a countdown of her own. Greta didn't know what to say without saying too much. "I should go. My brother's waiting."

"Okay. Why don't you give me your number? I'll text you, and you can text me back if you ever want to talk."

Slim chance of that. Greta wasn't sure anything she put in writing wouldn't be forwarded to every phone in the school. Still, she told Priya the number and watched her add it to her contact list. Why not? Rachel and Dylan already had it.

"Okay." The phone might get disconnected anyway, unless Roger had continued paying the bill. "See you." Greta turned and walked away before it got any more twilight zone.

She watched Priya during lunch, sitting beside Rachel, teasing Matt about something. Was she for real? Funny that when she wanted to, Priya knew just where to find her. Angus had probably said something about being in the same class. It wasn't that Greta had outsmarted them, crouching behind the ficus tree and taking back hallways; they just didn't care. It could all be much worse. Nobody harassed her online, telling her to kill herself, or beat her up in the girls' bathroom. She'd had her fifteen minutes of fame, and then things got quiet. Like, invisible-quiet.

Ash followed her eyes to them. Dylan wrestled with Chloe when she tried to shove a french fry up his nose, his arms around her body as he pinned her. Rachel reclined in Matt's lap. Priya and Sam chatted with a few new unknowns. Ash's face darkened, watching them, and he twitched in his seat. Greta didn't think he'd ever forgive them for what had happened after the party at the cabin. She looked away.

NINE

After school, they hesitated outside Elgin's door. "Do we knock?" Greta asked.

Ash raised his hand to knock before dropping it back by his side. "I don't know. We're supposed to live here now. Won't it drive him crazy, us knocking every time we come or go? He'll have to come to the door in that weird outfit."

"You're right." She pushed the door open, sliding off her boots on the mat. "Hello! We're home!" She didn't want to surprise him walking past in anything *less* than an undershirt and fluorescent running shorts.

From behind a fern at the kitchen table, Elgin lifted his head and waved. Ash and Greta hung out in their bedroom for an hour, the smell of something fantastic wafting under the door.

"How's this supposed to work?" Ash asked, peering over the side of the bed at Greta. She sat cross-legged with her homework spread out around her. He lowered his voice to a near whisper. "Do we cook for ourselves? Can we use his food? A job for every meal? I don't get it."

Greta shrugged. "I don't know. I guess we'll find out."

At five o'clock Elgin knocked on their door before opening it a crack. "Supper's ready, if you are."

When he left, Greta raised an eyebrow at Ash. They followed Elgin, the heat from the stove making the kitchen and living room even warmer. Condensation covered the windows, smudging their view of the darkening sky. Elgin pointed to the empty chairs at the table. He'd already set places for them, with a pot of rice and a wok filled with steak strips and grilled vegetables in the middle. Greta tried not to dive for her fork.

"Thank you. This looks fantastic," she said, torn between ravenous and awkward. They all sat looking at each other, waiting for someone to make the first move.

"Well, dig in." Elgin waved a hand toward the food.

Greta dished up, taking half of what she actually wanted before handing the spoons to Ash. He did the same and passed them to Eglin.

After one bite, Ash asked, "So how do we pay for meals?"

Greta wondered the same thing. One chore for basic carbohydrates? Two for any meal containing meat? Do twenty push-ups?

Elgin's eyebrows pressed together. "Sit, relax, eat," he said. "You aren't servants here." He finished dishing up his own food before speaking again. "My daughter, Alice, only comes by once a month. I like cooking and rarely have someone to cook for, so"—he gestured to the food again—"please eat it."

"Ash likes cooking too," Greta said. Ash looked at her, the sense of betrayal clear on his face. She didn't know why she'd said it. Must've been the steak. "Well, he used to." She put a large forkful in her mouth so she didn't have to speak again.

"That right?" Elgin said. "Maybe we can cook together sometime." He didn't seem to notice the color on Ash's cheeks or his murderous glare at Greta.

After Ash went into personal lockdown, Greta made small talk with Elgin. He had one daughter—Alice—and had taken an early retirement from Canada Post. "I'm waiting for spring," he said, looking over his shoulder at the kitchen window facing the backyard, "to put in my garden." He stared at the foggy black rectangle for an uncomfortable amount of time.

After dinner Greta tried to wash the dishes, but Elgin waved her away. "You kids take care of this"—he pointed at the fat flakes falling outside the window—"and I'll do the dishes. The shovel's by the front porch."

In their bedroom, they made a plan. Greta would shovel the walk first, before bed, and Ash would do it in the morning before going to school. And they'd do a good job, to pay for the steak.

Greta started to say, "Ash, I'm sorry—"

The door swung open wide, whacking Ash's cardboard box behind it. A woman a few years older than Ash and Greta stood with her arms and legs wide, ready for a shoot-out. They shrank from her long blond hair, upturned nose and frown lines on her forehead—Cinderella meets biker chick. Her nostrils flared as she looked back and forth between them.

Like she would either start singing to forest creatures or kick someone in the 'nads.

"Who are you?" she barked. Ash opened his mouth, but before he could answer she said, "And why in the holy hell do you think you can live at my dad's house for free?"

Alice.

"We're..." Greta started but trailed off when Alice's eyes burned her.

"You think this is this some kind of a shelter?" Alice asked, her voice fake-kind. "Are you comfortable in my old room?"

Elgin appeared at her elbow. "I told you already." He sighed. "Their parents abandoned them."

"And why is this *my* problem?" Alice asked, turning to look at him.

"Alice!" Elgin scolded.

"No, really. Who are these people?"

"A little humanity, please," he said.

She scoffed. "This, from you."

Ash pushed himself off the bed, a textbook clunking to the floor. "We plan to pay. We're both looking for jobs and waiting for our aunt to get back from Arizona." Greta knew that voice—the calm before the storm. "We're fully aware this isn't a shelter." He stepped close to her and pulled himself up tall. Somehow Alice seemed taller.

"And this future hypothetical money is supposed to help me how?" she asked. Ash's between-the-eyes line matched Alice's forehead lines.

"What does this have to do with you?" Ash asked, his calm shifting closer to storm.

"My dad uses that rent money to support me—his *daughter*—while I'm in school, genius." Alice spat out the words. "So you are literally robbing me with this Robin Hood act."

Ash's chest swelled. Elgin tugged on Alice's arm. "I have some money in savings," he said. "We'll figure it out."

Guilt dampened Greta's desire to claw out Alice's eyes. They had put Elgin in an awkward position. It wasn't like he was independently wealthy. In this tornado of fury, he was the only one who looked small.

Alice's head snapped back and forth between Elgin and Ash, her loose curls twitching down her back. "This isn't over," she said, turning and clomping down the hallway. They stood frozen as the front door slammed.

Elgin started to apologize, but Greta waved it away. "We'll have money soon. We're the ones who are sorry." She glanced over at Ash, who definitely didn't look sorry.

Elgin disappeared into his bedroom. Greta closed their door again, with Ash still poised for a fight.

"Wow. Finally someone who can out-badass you, Ash," she said. "Are you in love?"

. · · . ·

"I'm making lamb kebabs for dinner," Elgin said. "They're Alice's favorite."

"That's nice." If Ash was trying to sound excited, he was failing.

Greta had avoided the topic of Alice since she'd burst into their room a week earlier. She noticed Ash and Elgin had done the same.

"I could use your help making the rub," Elgin said. Ash didn't stop pulling clean silverware from the dishwasher and sorting it into a drawer. He pursed his lips tightly.

"Are you sure you don't want to save that for when Alice comes?" Greta asked, sliding clean plates onto a shelf.

"Oh, she's coming," Elgin said.

Ash and Greta stopped moving.

Elgin straightened and looked at them. "She's my daughter, and we need to make peace here."

Greta heard: *That monster is my spawn, and I plan to feed you to her.* "Ash and I could go downstairs for a while, if you want some alone time." Only one person had responded to Elgin's rental ad, and nothing had come of it. She and Ash had also applied for a few more jobs that week but hadn't heard anything back. They checked the answering machine in the basement every day. Greta had hoped to have everything lined up before they saw Alice again.

"No, that's not the point," Elgin said. "We need to sit down, all together, and sort this out. The ancient Greeks had a word for it—*heuristic.* It's not solving the problem completely but finding a functional solution."

Greta had the feeling a heuristic with Alice would involve a lot of yelling.

Elgin talked Ash through the recipe for the lamb. At first Ash barely looked at the bowl or teaspoon as he dumped in the paprika.

"A little more precision there," Elgin said, ignoring—or not noticing—Ash's scowl.

Then Ash measured out some thyme, basil, cumin and curry powder. He moved a little slower, his face relaxing.

"And here's the secret ingredient," Elgin said, passing Ash a packet of what looked like Shake 'n Bake chicken coating.

Ash eyed it before sprinkling some on top. "There you go." He slid the bowl toward Elgin and brushed off his hands. Then he washed pots in the sink and pretended not to watch Elgin as he massaged the spices into the raw lamb.

Ash disappeared as soon as the skewers went in the oven. Greta knew then she wouldn't apologize again for pushing him into the kitchen. It would be like Ash apologizing for pressuring her to go to school. It was the way things should be.

"Now, baby potatoes or rice?" Elgin asked Greta.

"I vote for potatoes." Dinner conversation might be an act-of-God disaster, but the food would taste great.

Greta and Ash were hiding in their room when Alice arrived. They heard her voice in the kitchen, and Elgin called them out a minute later. Greta hardly noticed the grilled lamb arranged on a platter in the middle of the table. Alice sat on Elgin's right side, her arms folded on the table like a Mafia boss. Greta had already coached Ash to stick to head nodding or shaking. Alice probably knew somebody who could make people disappear, no questions asked.

Greta said hello and Ash nodded as they slipped into their chairs.

Then it got quiet. No one spoke for a while, besides the odd comment from Alice, like "You feed freeloaders well, Dad" or "This tastes great—just lacking a little shame is all." Greta noticed Ash gripping his fork like a caveman discovering utensils for the first time. But he followed Greta's rules and didn't speak.

Then Elgin cleared his throat. "I think we should talk about this...situation."

And Alice talked. "Any jobs yet?" They shook their heads. "How convenient."

"We're trying," Greta said, breaking her own rule.

"You're obviously not trying hard enough. Have you even made résumés? You know you have to apply for more than one job, right?"

Ash glowered over his lamb kebabs. "Really? I thought people would come knock on our door and offer *us* jobs."

"You think you're funny? You think *this* is funny?"

"Okay, okay." Elgin waved his hands to calm them. "I'm sure something will work out soon."

Now Greta gripped her fork too and shot Ash a look. The more he talked, the more she wanted to kill Alice. *Stop it.*

"For your information," Ash said, ignoring Greta, "we do a lot to earn our way here, like grocery shopping, snow shoveling and cleaning."

"And how exactly is that helping me?" Alice snapped.

"Okaaaaay," Elgin said. His smooth tone a gravelly patch.

Alice threw up her hands, pushed back her chair and stomped to the door. She slipped onto the front porch with a cigarette and lighter from her purse.

"Sorry," Greta told Elgin, who had dropped his head in his hands, his food barely touched.

Elgin shook his head. "Ever since Eleanor died, I can't win," he said.

"Eleanor?" Greta asked.

"My wife. Alice's mother." His voice failed at the end of *mother*, and he ducked his head farther away from them.

It was bloody awful. Pantless Elgin, who fed them lamb, was possibly crying. Because they had moved in and had no money. And his wife had died. Plus his daughter was a freak. Greta pushed back her chair. She'd fix it somehow.

"Stay here," she told Ash. She'd do whatever it took.

Greta slipped on her shoes and stepped onto the porch. Alice twitched her head in Greta's direction before blowing a puff of smoke into the still air. The porch light shone over icing-sugar dunes. Alice didn't speak. Her eyes looked glassy-fragile too, like her dad's.

"Look, I'm so sorry," Greta said, "for how this has inconvenienced you. I want you to know we'll do whatever it takes to make it right." Then she braced herself.

"Okay." Alice nodded but still wouldn't look at Greta. Was that it?

Alice's face contorted as she tried to hold in tears. "He hasn't been functional in four years, and when he finally steps up, it's for someone else's kids." She shook away the tears, her face hardening again.

"Is that when your mom died? Four years ago?"

Scary Alice returned, her eyes scorching Greta.

"Your dad...said something...but I don't really know... anything," Greta stammered.

"Yes, that's when my mom died." She said it like it was Greta's fault.

"My mom died too. Nine years ago."

"You shitting me?"

"You think I'd pretend-kill my own mother?"

Some hackles lowered. "How'd she die?"

"Breast cancer," Greta said.

"Are you making this up to attempt to bond with me?"

Greta reached for the door, turning away before she could grab that cigarette and put it out on Alice's forehead. "You narcissistic—"

"Whoa, wait. Your mother died of breast cancer too?"

Greta nodded.

Alice faced her now, scanning Greta's eyes like she was trying to figure out if Greta was a real human or a cyborg. "You said your parents left. I thought that meant your mom too."

"My dad and evil stepmother."

While they stood there regarding each other, the door creaked open and Ash slipped through. Greta tried not to sigh at his bad timing. The tiny window of humanity Greta had seen opening in Alice banged shut.

"Hey," Ash said.

Alice practically sneered.

"I'll be in soon," Greta hinted, nudging him toward the door. "We're just...talking."

"Why are you so hard on your dad?" Ash asked.

Alice looked like she wanted to karate chop him with some scorching retort, but then sighed and dropped the cigarette butt on the porch, grinding it under her heel. "You've got to understand that after my mom died, my dad turned into this weird, pantless recluse you see now. Think anyone ever drops by for a barbecue or invites us over on Christmas?"

"I thought the lack of pants was heat related," Greta said.

"Yes," Alice answered. "And when summer rolls around, it will also be 'heat related.'

"I was sweating like a whore in church when he actually agreed to come to my high school graduation, like I'd turn around and find him talking to the plants or reciting haikus about death at the punch bowl."

Greta could picture Alice, in a too-puffy dress, gripping his arm. *Don't talk to anyone.* Greta nodded. Elgin was a little startling.

Ash kicked a clump of snow off the porch, pocking a flawless drift on the lawn. After a minute he said, "But he's here, giving you checks every month to support you. Making you lamb kebabs because they're your favorite. He's still lapping *our* dad."

"This isn't some dysfunctional-father contest," Alice said, but her voice had lost its steel.

Greta rubbed her bare arms, finally feeling the cold. "Why don't we try to finish dinner?" Greta said. "We can be civil for twenty minutes and kill each other after."

"I might take you up on that," Alice said. Greta couldn't tell if she was joking.

They sat down at the table again and stayed nearly silent for the next ten minutes. Elgin took this as an invitation to talk about Alice. Alice in school to become a dental assistant, Alice's ex-boyfriend (which earned him a frightening glare), Alice who had won Ping-Pong trophies, Alice who had been on the honor roll in junior high school.

When Elgin paused for a breath, Ash looked back and forth between Alice and Elgin and asked, "So…are you adopted?"

Greta almost kicked him under the table, except she was kind of wondering about the age difference herself. She thought Roger looked old, but Elgin definitely tipped the scale toward senior citizen.

"No, he's my biological father," Alice said in a voice that told Greta she'd had this conversation a million times. "He was twenty years older than my mom, and she's the one who died first. Consider the irony."

After dinner, they watched a rerun of *Quiz Kings*. And no one talked about jobs or rent or dead mothers. When Alice grabbed her jacket to leave, she pointed back and forth between Ash and Greta. "When I come back, I expect you to tell me about your new jobs."

They nodded dumbly, even Ash. One did not poke a rabid wolverine with a stick. Not more than once anyway.

TEN

They told Nate about Alice on the ride to school the next day.

"I missed out on all the fun?" Nate laughed.

"She's a complete psycho. That's what you missed," Ash said.

"You forgot to mention she looks like Cinderella," Greta added. "Cinderella who has spent a lot of time at boot camp."

Nate slumped in the driver's seat. "Maybe I can come next time."

Why not throw Nate in the mix? They could play a game of Would You Rather while Alice uttered death threats and Elgin modeled his collection of vintage running shorts. They could even combine the two, and Alice could make them choose between creative ways to die. *Would you rather douse yourself in lighter fluid and volunteer to carry the Olympic torch or hang upside down over a river of crocodiles by a bungee cord made of plastic shopping bags?*

Later that morning, on her way to lunch, Greta was thinking about their dinner with Alice and how to come up with some money ASAP. She bent over for a drink at a water fountain in the "safe" hallway. As she stood up, she nearly plowed into Rachel. Real Rachel this time, with her glossy black hair and a cute little shirt. Rachel stumbled back onto Matt's toes, surprise stealing any expression from their faces for a second. Dylan and Chloe followed a few steps behind, his arm slung over her shoulder. It was the at-school-in-your-underwear dream. A root canal without freezing. Every bad thing all at once.

Matt reacted first, looking as if he smelled something bad. Rachel's eyes examined the lockers, top to bottom. Dylan and Chloe sauntered up and stopped. Dylan tried not to laugh, and Chloe had an *I won, loser* smile. Greta repented of every bad thought she'd ever had about Priya and Angela. This was how it felt to be on the other side.

Dylan stepped forward, pushing past Matt and Rachel. His face got serious, leaning in close. She recoiled, the water fountain digging into her leg. Adrenaline buzzed in every limb, her heart pounding. She had once wanted that face close to hers, wanted to touch that body. Now his proximity scorched her.

"Boo!" he whispered. Then he stepped back, laughing. Chloe and Matt sniggered. Rachel's face reddened.

Priya walked up behind them and took it all in—Greta shrinking from their cold laughter. She had missed the words but understood everything. "Grow up, you guys." She cuffed Matt and Dylan on the backs of their heads. "Four against one isn't even fair." Her eyes held Greta's for a second before moving past, pulling them all forward.

Their laughter shifted to something else, Greta already forgotten.

The tears came before she made it to the bathroom. She'd tried. She'd really tried. On the Sunday after the party, Greta had only left her room a couple of times, and always wearing a turtleneck. She'd scrubbed her body in the shower, the water scalding hot, and shrunk from her limp clothes on the bathroom floor. Like they were infected by deadly bacteria and needed to be burned rather than just washed. After her shower she'd shoved them deep into the laundry hamper in her bedroom. But somehow she'd still sensed them there— not far enough away. Later, when everyone slept, she dug out the shirt, wrapped it in a plastic bag and dropped it in the garbage can behind the house. No one would find it there.

Sunday night, lying in bed, Greta gave herself a pep talk. In the tally of reliefs and embarrassments, embarrassments won by a landslide. Could she even salvage this? Getting blind drunk on half of what anyone else had consumed. And who knew how she'd been with Dylan. He'd had a lot of girlfriends, then her—the drunk virgin. Was she terrible? Being too sick to help clean up the next morning, not saying more than three words to anyone. Greta pressed her face into her pillow to quash the squirming. Monday would be a Reset button. She'd feel better, dress nice. Act normal. Smile. Maybe they'd laugh about it.

But then Greta found out she didn't hold the Reset button. Angus—who Greta vaguely remembered hitting on her—came toward her on the way to English that Monday, giving her a cold stare before walking past. "That was easy," he said, close to her ear, meaning *you were easy.* In bio, Priya had watched her with unblinking cat eyes. Then Sam had clutched her arm in the bathroom, beaming. "I heard." Like there should be a Hallmark card for the occasion. In the hallway, a girl who sat with them at lunch smiled—really smiled. Greta didn't even know her name. A few others had darted glances at her when she walked down the hall. Did she imagine it? When she'd sat down next to Rachel at lunchtime, though, Chloe got up and left. The table felt even emptier with Matt and Dylan at a lunchtime intramurals game.

It was funny—a few weeks earlier, no one had known she existed. Now everything about her was defined by Dylan's penis, her contact with it and whether people approved or disapproved.

When Greta and Rachel had stopped by their lockers at the end of the lunch hour, Greta pulled Rachel aside, trying to sort out her head. "I think I made a mistake, that it was too soon. I don't know." She stared at a spot on the floor.

Rachel put her hand on Greta's arm. "You like Dylan, right?"

Greta nodded.

"And he likes you. So what's the problem?"

"I—" It was hard to explain. She'd imagined it all differently. She didn't even know if she'd liked it, his body on hers. "It was my first time, and…"

"Oh, really?" Rachel cringed. She grabbed Greta's other arm too. "Don't worry. Drunk sex is the worst. It gets better.

I promise." Greta watched Rachel's eyes look past her shoulder, and she turned to see Ash, holding out her English textbook.

"I took this by accident," he said. Then he'd left, his face blank.

Panic had strangled Greta again, the feeling she'd tried to corral all weekend. Everything had spilled out of her control. "He didn't hear that, did he?"

Rachel shrugged. "I'm not sure. I don't think so."

Greta watched his head disappear down the hall.

"Are you worried about your brother finding out?"

"Kind of. It's embarrassing." But not quite. Embarrassing was when she didn't have the right clothes or lived in a dumpy stucco basement suite. This reduced her to something less than human. *Shame, shame, double shame, now we know your boyfriend's name.*

"You're overthinking this." Rachel put her free hand around Greta's waist and led her back into the busy stream of the hallway. "This is all very normal."

Rachel was right. It happened all the time. *It's what's done.* And she had just compounded her weekend awkwardness by making an even bigger deal of it. Greta's body felt hollow, from her center right into her legs. She realized she'd been looking for the right words, the right gesture—from someone, anyone—to make it right. She drifted, unanchored, from class to class.

After school, Rachel had stopped by her locker. "So I was talking to Matt and Dylan, and we're thinking of going out to the cabin again this Saturday."

The cabin. The words fell into the hollow, stirred up something inside Greta.

When Rachel asked, "Are you interested in coming?" Greta had thought that was it, her reset.

"I'll come," she'd said.

But it hadn't gone as planned, hadn't been her reset. And today, as she'd cowered against a water fountain, Dylan had smashed her insides again with one word. Inside a bathroom stall, she took deep breaths, trying to pull herself back to a state to be seen in public. *I've got to get out of here. Ash.* She needed him, that pillar by her side. But couldn't tell him. She waited until the bell rang at the end of the lunch hour, and the bathroom and hallways emptied. Then she pressed cold paper towels against her eyes and slipped a note into Ash's locker about feeling sick and leaving early.

Outside, the cold soothed her inflamed face. She closed her eyes and let the swelling calm. After scrounging in her backpack for change, she waited fifteen minutes for the bus.

On the path in front of Elgin's house, Greta eyed the doors to the upper and lower suites. She didn't want the basement—the memory of it full of mold and shadows— but upstairs she'd be with Elgin, in his barely there running outfit, by herself. He seemed harmless. She hadn't caught him staring at her breasts or acting like a creeper. Still. She tromped an arrow in the snow, pointing to the basement, so Ash would know where to find her.

Greta slipped through the basement door, quietly, to avoid waking any ghosts. Her eyes adjusted to the grayish shapes, slowly making sense of them again: a boxy sofa, the thin line of a floor lamp, the lump of a discarded blanket. Cold and musty—an abandoned space. She didn't even bother lighting the oven, wrapping herself in a blanket on the sofa instead.

She could never make sense of those shards still rattling loose inside her. They dug in, but no matter how long she looked at them, they never formed a whole picture. A grotesque kaleidoscope. When she tried to sort through it, all the colors mixed together until it turned into a swamp brown.

. · · · .

The second night at the cabin was supposed to fix everything. Just her, Rachel, Matt and Dylan. No Priya in a little black dress. No Angus trying to move in when Dylan turned his back.

"We have dibs on the good bed tonight," Matt had said from the front seat of Rachel's car, looking over his shoulder at Dylan.

"We'll see about that," Dylan said, nudging Greta.

She laughed, a tinny sound that grated in her ears. It would take some drinks. Maybe not the toxic punch that nearly killed her. But something.

Greta knew the turns in the road now, the signs they were close. The old boulder of nausea wobbled in her gut. She ignored it, unbuckling her seat belt the moment they pulled into the driveway. Matt collected some loose beer cans rolling around the car floor while Rachel pulled a plastic shopping bag from the trunk.

It hadn't snowed since the weekend before. Their old tracks and footprints still marked the driveway and porch. Greta stepped close to Dylan on the cabin deck, suddenly chilled. The cabin would be cold.

Matt stumbled past, leaning close to the deck to drop the cans spilling from his arms onto a cushion of snow. He peeled back the welcome mat for the key. A plastic baggie sat on the bare deck boards, something white inside. He picked it up and felt underneath. No key.

"What the hell is this?" Matt ripped the seal of the baggie open and pulled a slip of paper from inside. *"Did you really think we wouldn't find out you had a party?"* he read. He swore and dropped the bag and paper in the snow, then turned and started pacing. Kicked a dead potted plant into the snow. "How'd they know?"

Matt checked the door and lower windows, which they all knew was pointless. "And they were all *have a nice night!* when I left," he said. "Unbelievable."

They stood there looking at each other.

"So," Rachel said, "should we hang out in the car? The shed? Turn around and go home?" She ran her fingers through her hair.

Not home. How could Greta have a reset if they went home now?

"Maybe we can get into one of these empty cabins," Matt said, looking around. "Climb in a window or something."

"No way," Rachel said. "Do I look like a felon?"

"You guys do what you like," Dylan said, scooping two beer cans from the snow. "I know where Greta and I are going."

Where are we going?

"See you in an hour," Dylan said. "Do you have a blanket in your car, Rachel?"

Matt snorted. "An hour. More like ten minutes."

Dylan ignored him, and Rachel pulled a blanket from the trunk. He draped it across his and Greta's shoulders as they walked in the direction of the only cabin with a porch light—a mobile home that resembled someone's giant junk drawer: whirligigs, lawn gnomes, plastic flowers. The whole line of cabins looked a little haunted, with their dark windows along the gravel road and the one stark light. Bare trees in a brisk wind.

Behind them, the car doors opened and closed. Their feet crunched the brittle ice of melted and refrozen snow. Across from the mobile home, Dylan led her under the branches of the large pine and along the side of an empty log cabin. They put their hands out to feel their way, entirely blocked from any light. "It's just up ahead," Dylan said.

The moonlight outlined the branches of an apple tree—the yard a mushy gray—and the rooftops of a shed and garage. "Up here." Dylan pulled her forward and helped boost her onto the shed roof, then pulled himself up. They crossed over to the garage roof, crouching close to the snow-covered shingles. He spread out the blanket and sat down, cracking a can of beer and handing it to her.

She took a sip, her stomach clenching against the memory of the previous week. From the garage roof, the other cabins formed a dark collage of shapes. Cold seeped through the blanket beneath her. The air had stayed just cool enough to maintain the snow. A flirtation with winter up to this point. She leaned against Dylan's shoulder, and he reached for her hand.

"How was your week?" she asked him.

Dylan laughed. "You want to talk about basketball?"

Anything about him, actually. Who did he come home to? What did he worry about, and who worried about him?

Dylan took the can from her hand and set it by his, precariously angled on the roof. He eased her back, so she rested her head on his chest. The heat from his body made up for the damp blanket.

He traced his thumb along her hip bone where the bare skin and belt loop met. Cold but somehow scalding where he touched. She knew it began now. His hand on her belly, then moving up her shirt. She became still—not even breathing— and felt herself shrink next to his body, suddenly immense. He pressed against her side. Reaching over, he took her palm and held it against his chest, sliding it down his abs, lower. She pulled her hand away and ran it up his back. His body shifted onto her, crushing. She needed the beer just out of reach. Even Matt's toxic punch. Something. He bent to kiss her while he fumbled with the button on her jeans, tugging them over her hips. *It's what's done.*

Her lungs collapsed, imploding under his weight. Held under water too long. Arms that weren't her own pushed against his body. She wormed out from beneath him, off the blanket and into the snow. Gasped for air. Dylan sat up on his elbows, unbalanced.

"What? What's wrong?" he asked.

"I don't know." Her face burned. "I'm sorry. I just... can't...right now."

He pulled himself to sitting and faced her, a gray form in the dark. "I don't understand. Was I hurting you?"

"No." Not exactly. Just pressing the life from her.

"It's just...you seemed to want it last weekend."

"Did I?" It was a relief to speak the words out loud. She needed to know. *What did I say? What did I do? Can you tell me?*

"Whoa. What are you implying?"

"Nothing. I just don't...know...what happened."

"You're saying you didn't want to sleep with me?" Anger hardened his voice—the first time she'd heard it there.

She tried to say no, then yes, but nothing fit. All the words jumbled in her head and wouldn't line up in a sentence.

"I get it." He jumped to his feet and strode to the edge of the garage.

Greta scrambled after him, buttoning her jeans. "Wait! Where are you going?"

He covered the shed roof in one step and hopped to the ground. Greta slipped on the tinny slope and caught herself. She lowered to a squat and jumped, landing hard on her right ankle.

"Dylan!"

"I can't believe you!" His voice came from along the side of the cabin now, out of sight.

"Wait!"

He didn't answer, but she could hear his heavy steps on the gravel. Her ankle pulsed. She hobbled to catch up. Along the dark side of the cabin, under the pine tree, onto the road. Up ahead, the night nearly swallowed his shadow. The car's interior light flashed on, Dylan holding the door handle. Rachel's voice from inside.

By the time Greta caught up, Dylan, Matt and Rachel all stood outside the car—both doors hanging wide open. Matt gave her a cold stare, arms crossed over his chest. Rachel looked back and forth between Greta and Dylan, frowning.

Dylan turned and faced Greta. Three against one. "I liked you," he said. "And then you accuse me of being some kind of…predator."

"I didn't!"

"I know what I heard. I'm done." He motioned for Rachel and Matt to get in the car.

Greta moved forward, toward her spot behind Rachel.

"No!" Dylan held out his arm, blocking her way. "You can find your own way home."

"Dylan—" Rachel stepped beside him and touched his shoulder. He shook her off. Matt didn't say anything, flipping the passenger seat forward for Dylan to climb into the back.

"Rachel"—Greta didn't recognize her own voice, high and frantic—"Rachel, don't leave me here!"

Dylan turned and stared Rachel down. "Get in the car. Drive."

Matt called, "Get in, Rachel. She'll find another ride."

Rachel looked at Greta, then at the ground. Like she might vomit. She turned, walked to the driver's side and climbed in. When the engine hummed, Dylan backed away from Greta and ducked into the seat behind Matt.

The car rolled forward for a second, then peeled away, tires spinning on ice.

"Don't leave…!" They were gone before she could say *me*. She chased the car, but the taillights rounded the bend, out of sight. Darkness closed in on her.

She had wanted Dylan, wanted to be with him, wanted to touch him. Why had she slept with him and then said no to him? She'd wrecked it. It was stupid, made no sense at all. On top of it all, bleeding into everything, shame, guilt. They whispered, *Don't tell. Your fault.* But Dylan, Matt and Rachel had left her in the middle of nowhere—a temper tantrum—and ignored her and treated her like a pariah. Couldn't they own that?

ELEVEN

Ash found her in the basement suite. "Why don't you come upstairs now?" he said, standing over her. "You can have my bed. I have some cleaning to do, but I'll be around."

Greta followed him up the flight of stairs and walked to their bedroom, no sign of Elgin. Ash pulled out a mop and bucket from a broom closet by the bathroom. Greta climbed into Ash's empty bed and read until early dusk dimmed the sunlight. She heard the television turn on in the living room. Not wanting to attract attention, then conversation, she left the light off.

Elgin tapped on her door sometime after 7:00 PM, "Greta? I've put a plate in the fridge for you, in case you feel better."

She wanted to thank him, but that would confirm she was awake and possibly lead to more talking. She played on her phone under the covers instead, her stomach growling.

A couple of hours later Ash came back, and Greta climbed into her own bed. When she heard him drop onto his mattress, she said, "Goodnight, Ashwin."

"Just Ash is good."

"Did you know that Ashwin means 'light' and 'brave knight' and 'friend' and 'protector'? I googled it today."

Ash snorted. "Really?"

"Kind of fitting, don't you think?"

"I would say more ironic, in my case."

"No, Ash." They didn't speak for a few minutes. And then she said, "The name Greta means 'pearl.'"

"Hmm. I bet Mom picked those."

She nodded back, even though he couldn't see her. *Brave knight* did seem unlike Roger. He would've come up with something like Chuck or Bob. After a few minutes, when Ash's breathing slowed, Greta slid from under her blankets and pushed herself to her feet. Her growling stomach wouldn't let her forget the plate of food in the fridge. And her thirst. She licked her dry lips.

The fridge light brightened the kitchen as she opened the door and reached for a covered plate on the top shelf. Greta peeled back the plastic wrap, knowing she couldn't risk the beep of the microwave. Even cold, the lasagna still smelled delicious. After drinking two glasses of water, she grabbed a fork on the way to the living room and then settled in one of the armchairs facing the window. So easy to watch winter this way—observing the pristine white through a pane of glass. She could wade out into it, she thought—it wouldn't even feel cold.

"Feeling better?"

Greta fumbled the plate, nearly dropping it into her lap. Elgin, reclined in the other chair, smiled through the glow of streetlights.

"Yes, I had a…long nap." She cleared her throat and took a bite. "Thanks for this." Then her heartbeat picked up and the lasagna stuck in her throat. They were alone—Elgin just a few feet from her, wearing only a bathrobe.

She put the plate on the end table between them, keeping the fork hidden in her hand. *Get out of here*, her body told her. *He's fine. He's harmless*, her mind answered.

Elgin nodded, looking satisfied. He turned back to his snow observation.

She clutched the fork. If he moved at all in her direction, she'd stick it in his knee. She'd scream for Ash. Only her body was frozen. *You're not staying here for free.* The thought overpowered all the others. *He'll want something from you.* For a few minutes, they sat in silence, both completely still—inanimate objects. Elgin didn't even look her way. Greta thought of Ash sleeping close by and started breathing again, her heartbeat slowing closer to normal.

She moved to the edge of her seat but didn't run. "What… what are you doing out here?" Greta couldn't think of another way to say it.

"I'm waiting for spring."

How very Elgin, sitting in an armchair, literally waiting for spring. "You have a few months," she said.

"It doesn't look like it"—he cocked his head—"but every day we rotate a little closer to the sun. It's coming."

He was right about it not looking like spring. More like the inside of a diamond mine. An unholy blackness. It had always been February. That a garden once grew there, that they swatted mosquitoes, sunburned red rings around their necks—all an elaborate dream. An implanted memory. It would always be February.

When Greta didn't respond, he added, "Eleanor and I liked to put in the garden early. I could never talk her into waiting until after the May long weekend."

Maybe Elgin did feel it, a gradual shift every day. It comforted her.

Then he said, "Since Eleanor left us, I don't sleep well at night."

Left us. She'll be right back. Greta nodded. "Did Alice tell you we lost our mom to breast cancer too?"

"Yes. I'm sorry." His voice barely made it past the fern leaves on the end table between them.

They sat without speaking for several minutes, watching a few chiseled flakes pass through the circle of porch light.

"For me," Greta said, "it's not so much the sleeping as the waking." Her heart and breath had slowed to normal now, her brain processing thoughts again. Elgin hadn't even turned in her direction.

"Yes, the waking." He knew. "For one blessed moment," he said, "you're a blank slate. Then your mind looks around, bends over and picks up that bag of misery to carry around another day."

Bag of misery. That daily three-second shift from peace to distress.

"And willing the mind not to only makes it happen faster," he added. "It runs, in that case."

She gave a soft laugh. "Yes." The luggage they never lost.

"Though," he mused, "sometimes I wonder."

"What do you wonder?"

"I wonder...if this is the dream, and that's reality. Perhaps we're dreaming now."

"Why do you say that?"

Elgin turned back to the window, studying the stark black and white of night. "This can't be it. I won't accept it. I refuse it, in fact." Grief hardened his gentle voice. "Impossible that this is the real world."

Greta wanted to say something comforting, like this was the real world but beauty still existed, or remind him to think of what he still had—Alice, his health and whatnot. It's what she'd been trained to do, to fill absurd, painful spaces with polite phrases. But his words sunk into her skin and fit so well. Elgin was right. This had to be the dream. Unacceptable as reality. Totally unacceptable.

She rejected it too.

, ˙ ˙ ˙ ,

Ash stood over her, nudging her with his foot. "Are you still sick?" Black morning and streetlights showed through the crack in the curtain.

Blank slate. For one second, just her and Ash, like every morning for seventeen years. Then her mind bent over and picked up the bag of misery. It spilled over into her arms, slid down her legs, suffocated her with its weight. *Mom. Roger.*

Patty. Gone. Money. Jobs. Alice. Cancer. Elgin. Dylan. Rachel. Cabin. Water fountain. She lay flat on her back and felt it press her body into the sagging air mattress, struggling for air.

"I'm not going to school anymore, Ash." No point in this pretense.

He twitched like he'd been shocked. "What are you talking about? We graduate in four months."

"I'm done." Every word she spoke carried weight off her body. To give in to those words, concede, walk away—that allowed her to breathe. She actually felt happy. No, elated.

"Why are you saying this?" Ash's voice tightened.

"I'll get a job. You go to school. I'll finish at some point, maybe in the fall." Dylan, Rachel and Matt would've graduated and moved on by then. It was a small price—practically nothing.

Ash looked down on her, his eyes just sockets in the dark room. "I'm not leaving here without you."

Her gut clenched. Could she make that decision for him too? Was he bluffing? "Okay. That's your call."

He stood beside her for another minute before walking out and slamming the door behind him, probably waking Elgin. After the vibration settled, she padded to the kitchen. Sunrise glowed over Elgin's garden boxes in the backyard, rounded in snow. She made two pieces of toast, a fried egg and a cup of tea, then pulled over a kitchen chair to face the window above the sink. The mug warmed her hands as she watched the orange and pink burn away the deep blue of night.

She missed this every morning—rushing for the bus, dodging through windowless hallways.

Elgin got up around noon and found her on the couch, playing a game on her phone. After their conversation the night before, it felt okay to be there. She still watched him walk by, though, not too close to her.

"Still not feeling well?" he asked, rubbing his porcupine hair. Today's shorts were white with sporty gray stripes down the sides, still ballooning around his plucked-chicken legs. His undershirt hung in a misshapen U around his neck.

"A little better today," Greta said. She would watch for the right time to explain her plan.

Elgin shuffled to the kitchen and turned on the coffee maker. "I got a check in the mail from your dad yesterday, by the way."

"You what?" She bolted upright.

"He mailed me a check. No note or letter with it, but it's enough to cover rent with a little left over. After Alice cashes it, I'll ask her to bring the extra back for you two, for incidentals and such."

Greta meant to answer him, to say thank you, but her mind started scanning all possible meanings and outcomes before she could speak. Roger hadn't sent the check to her and Ash directly—probably because neither one had a bank account—but he must've guessed they were still living there. He was thinking about them? In Whitecourt, he'd tried to tell them he'd send money. But what about Patty? Either she'd softened her "silver platter" stance or he'd done it secretly, which explained the rushed check in the mail and lack of a note. What did it mean?

. · · · .

Ash tried to walk into their bedroom after school, but the door whacked against the dresser Greta had pushed in front of it, although Elgin hadn't even spoken to her all afternoon. After she slid it aside to let Ash in, he gave her a look and asked, "Is there something I should know about Elgin, Greta?"

She shook her head, flopping back on the air mattress. "Just being…careful." *Paranoid*. When he didn't look away, she added, "I feel safer when you're around. By myself…" She didn't finish the sentence. Her logical brain wasn't scared of Elgin at all—an aging philosopher dressed as an eighties track star—but sometimes the other part took over.

Ash closed the door and leaned back against it. "I dropped all my classes," he said.

Greta sat up, her hand sinking into the mattress and tilting the book shut. "You did *what*?"

"I dropped my classes and joined yours. I'll go with you. Every day."

"But you already took French. Those credits won't count."

"Yeah, the guidance counselor seemed pretty annoyed. I told him I didn't get a high enough mark the first time…and I want to be a French teacher."

Greta barked a laugh. Ash, a teacher? He mostly avoided kids. Humans in general. And schools. And speaking.

"What about art?"

He shrugged. "I'll take it another time—maybe when I'm unemployed and going through an existential crisis in my twenties."

Greta lay on her back and filled her lungs. "Ash, you didn't have to do that."

"Yes, I did," he snapped. "I told you I'm not leaving you behind. It's just you and me...and kind of him"—he motioned to the kitchen and then across the street—"and him." Interesting. So Elgin and Nate stood on the periphery of their dysfunctional circle too.

"Will you have enough credits to graduate?"

"Barely."

"You idiot." She craned her neck forward to see him better, grinning.

"You're welcome."

"Thank you." Then she scrambled to face him, almost forgetting. "Ash, Dad sent a check to Elgin yesterday."

"He did?"

She watched his face, his mind probably running in the same directions as hers. "What do you make of it? It covers rent and a little bit extra for us."

He stared past her, his eyes unfocused. "Not sure. It takes some pressure off anyway. Maybe now Alice will stop coming around for her pound of flesh."

At that moment Elgin knocked and poked his head inside. "I nearly forgot to ask you," he said. "Now that your dad is sending money, I won't have to rent out the basement.

Did you"—he stammered over the words—"want to move back down there? It's still going to be chilly for another month or two."

Ash and Greta looked at each other for a second. "Nah," Ash said.

Greta paused. They could be back in their own space again—no dresser shoved against the door or old man legs. Still, when her body was calm, she felt, in some inexplicable way, safe with Elgin. His slow shuffling around his plants, or puttering in the kitchen, dreaming of an alternate universe where his wife was still alive. And just to have someone to care if they'd eaten supper or were warm enough at night. She looked from Ash to Elgin. "I think we're good here, if it's okay with you."

"All settled then." Elgin nodded and closed the door behind him.

. . . .

The next morning rocks tumbled in her belly, but they didn't crush her. Ash hovered like she might fall over.

In social studies, Greta sat right in front of Angus, the force of Ash at her side erasing Angus completely. She silently dared him to say something. She didn't even have to look at Ash—she felt him. Solid. Like that night, abandoned at the cabin.

She'd shuffled backward, looking in the direction Rachel had gone, afraid to miss their return, stumbling over the uneven ground. The mobile home of garden gnomes and pink flamingos the only light in the entire world. Maybe someone there. Greta had swiveled around, streaking for the shack, nighttime snapping at her heels. Everything not touched by that single porch light conspired against her.

She'd hammered on the door. Another human—that's what she needed. Another living being in the dark. Greta cringed at the racket of her knocking, a beacon for everything hiding in the shadows. She pounded again, checking over her shoulder, then slumped against it. Nothing. Entirely alone.

Greta tried to sort out her mind, her beating heart scattering every piece of clarity. Roger thought she was at Rachel's house. Who would find her out here? She'd smash a cabin window. She'd make a bonfire. She'd walk to the highway at first light. And the cold? Even after Roger's nagging, she'd only worn a stupid leather jacket instead of a real winter coat. And what about food? Water?

Greta's fingers brushed the hard corner of her phone in her jacket pocket, her relief a flare of light. People lived out here for months at a time—there had to be cell service. She pulled it out. One weak bar. She exhaled, dizzy.

Who to call? Her first stupid thought was Rachel. She closed her eyes. Roger would come for her. But then so many questions. He'd make her live at home until she was thirty. Only one person for this job. He'd be the one closest to the phone anyway, probably watching TV.

Greta made the phone call and then waited nearly an hour, huddled on the steps of the cabin with all the lawn junk.

If she stepped out of the light, wild animals, shadows, the boogeyman would snatch her. At one point she heard footsteps and turned round and round in a frantic circle, the phone light bobbing. But then nothing. Bushes rustled. The wind? Fear wrapped everything in a cold ball inside of her.

Ash pulled up, hunched over the wheel of Patty's rusty Honda Civic. She waved her arms, limping down the road to meet him. He parked and jumped out, the engine still running.

"Greta!"

She held herself back from hugging him, clinging. Even her sore ankle was numb now. Exhaustion nearly knocked her over—holding everything in so tight. She fell into the passenger seat and breathed in the warm air, the cloying peach air freshener, her eyes closed.

"Greta, what the hell is going on? What is this place?"

She ignored his eyes on her. "Just drive. I'll explain."

Ash watched her for a second before sighing, turning the car around and heading back the way he'd come.

"Patty will lose her freaking mind, you know," Ash said, "if she finds out I've taken her car. You're lucky they had a few drinks at bingo and wouldn't wake up for an earthquake."

Greta nodded, her eyes still closed.

"And I don't even have my full driver's license yet. Did you think of that? I'm taking the bus for the rest of my life if I get pulled over."

"Thank you, Ash."

Where the dirt road met the highway, he put the car into Park. "I'm not moving until you explain"—he motioned to the cabins, trees, lake—"*this*."

"I came out here with Rachel and some other people."

"And? Where are they?"

"Rachel thought I got a ride with someone else, and someone else thought I got a ride with Rachel." She kept her eyes shut tight. It felt unnatural, lying to Ash.

"They *left* you?" he shouted.

"Not on purpose."

"I don't care 'on purpose' or not! They left you!"

"Please, Ash. Just let it go. Promise me you won't say anything to Rachel."

"I will not promise that! What happened here is not okay!"

What happened here is not okay. Little did he know. Greta rolled her head to face the window.

When she didn't respond, Ash added, "Tell me you're not going to hang out with them on Monday like nothing happened."

"No, Ash." She talked so low, she wasn't sure he heard. "It's over." *Over. Over. Over. Over. How could it be anything but over?*

She held on tight all the way home, cracks spidering through whatever was holding her together. Through the door and into the unlit basement, Ash replacing Patty's keys and tiptoeing behind her. Held tight as she said goodnight and thank you. In her room, in bed, she sobbed. Her pillow pressed against her mouth.

She had followed Rachel, Dylan—all of them—taking whatever crumbs they threw her way, believing they would lead somewhere wonderful. Somewhere outside that basement suite and who she was there. Then she'd realized there was no trail, nothing offered. She had never moved at all.

TWELVE

Greta tried to shake the memory away, smiling at Ash as he thumbed through the social studies textbook. They didn't speak as they moved to their French class. Half an hour into the lesson, the principal made an announcement over the PA system, calling all classes to the gym for a school-wide pep rally. The senior boys' basketball team was headed to regionals the next day. "Bring your school spirit!" he crooned.

Ash arched an eyebrow at Greta and visually dismantled the PA speaker. "Let's stand near the door," he whispered. "Five minutes in, we both have to go to the bathroom—for a long time."

Greta followed at his shoulder to the gym, ushered by Madame Dubois and her hawk eyes. Through the double doors, some of the class broke off to fill the small spaces in the bleachers. Other students sat along the sides of the court or leaned against the wall. Ash staked out the exit, the gym teacher standing sentry. Greta felt Ash's arm twitch against hers. A pep rally of any kind would be water torture for Ash, each waving banner one drip closer to insanity. And this one would stink of Rachel and her cronies.

Ash and Greta leaned against the wall by the gym office, not far from the exit. Greta focused on the feet lining the base of the bleachers, shoes of every shape and color. The last time she'd sat in the gym and watched Dylan and Matt play, everything had been different. Now her eyes swept the bleachers, checking for Rachel twirling her black hair. There, in the top row, on the opposite side of the gym, Rachel sat with Sam, Priya, Chloe and some new faces. If things had been different—if Greta had been different—Greta would be there too.

Her eyes fell on a couple sitting in the bleachers to her right, their backs to her. A big guy dressed all in black stretched his arm around the waist of a girl with a bleached-blond pixie cut, his thumb hanging from her waistband. Then he slipped it under the bottom of her shirt, against her bare skin. She smiled tightly, twisted away from him and gave him a look. Greta tried to read the look from the girl's profile. *Not here*, it said. Maybe *Not at all*? He didn't move his hand though. The purple-punch feeling trickled through Greta. She couldn't look away.

The principal strode to the middle of the gym with a cordless mic and called for quiet, breaking Greta's trance. After talking for a minute about the team's successes through the season, he announced they would start the rally with a students-versus-teachers shoot-off. The basketball team jumped from their bench, hooting, arms bare in their jerseys. A few teachers trickled onto the court—the sacrificial lambs.

Dylan stepped forward for his team, first up. Cat calls and whistles erupted from every side. He motioned for them to go louder, and the bleachers rumbled with stomping feet.

"Why him?" Ash asked softly, somehow audible through the thunder. They watched Dylan strut around the gym, pumping his arm in the air. "Why him, Greta?" he asked again, turning to look at her.

His face close to hers. She fixed on the black ring circling his green irises, a burst of brown around the pupil. She knew. He knew. She knew he knew. *Why'd you sleep with this clown? Why him?*

His eyes locked her in place, grounded her. A moment of stillness in the waves of chaos rolling around them. The worst had happened—Ash knew—and they still stood there together.

"I didn't," she said. At hearing the lie, his sharp green eyes dulled and shifted to her ear. He looked down at the floor and back up, his face tired now. "I didn't"—the words left her mouth, bypassing her brain—"say yes."

I didn't say yes. Those four words ripped through her, blowing open doors and windows. Locking others. Everything a different color now. The whole story shifted. *I didn't say yes.*

For a moment, Greta was back in her bedroom, rolled in a blanket cocoon, while Ash dealt with Patty. She had sent him out to fight that battle, to deliver that ultimatum.

She stayed wrapped tightly, a step away from it all, as Ash launched onto the basketball court and tackled Dylan. She didn't call for him to stop, didn't ask for mercy, as Ash pinned

Dylan on his back and beat his face, again and again. She didn't move as bodies rushed to pull him off. Flecks of blood spattered the court. She said nothing at all.

When the howling of five hundred people reached her ears, and a wave of bodies lurched and heaved forward, Greta fled through the unguarded door. She ran, her feet slapping the floor of the empty hallway. At her locker, she yanked her coat and purse from the hook. Too risky to return the way she came—the crowd might spill from the gym any second and swallow her up. She felt their vibration chase her from the school.

At the door to the parking lot, Greta ducked out, checking over her shoulder. A buzz whispered in the distance, growing. She ran, scrambling on ice, to the sidewalk ringing the school. Arms pumping, her boots gripping the shoveled walks, she ran.

Ten minutes from the school, at a bus stop nearly hidden by a tree, Greta doubled over. Air seared her lungs—ice and fire. It couldn't come fast enough, and then it was gone before she could get enough. What had she done, leaving him to the mob? What had *he* done? She hadn't asked him to, didn't want that. Did she? *Maybe.* She smothered that admission. Why had she told him in the first place? The weight of it. Something that held those words distant—from Ash and herself—had broken loose. So heavy to carry. She should go back, stand beside him. Face any consequences with him. *Forgive me, Ash.*

Five minutes later Greta caught the first bus that pulled up, waving an old bus transfer. The driver looked at her face and pretended not to notice. They drove a city block before she even asked him where they were headed. The driver knew of a stop within walking distance of her house. Then she collapsed in a seat, her head knocking against the window.

Elgin. Today she couldn't even handle his quiet plant pruning. She ducked low, passing his picture window, and headed straight to the door of the basement suite.

She pulled a chair over to the oven, held a match near the stream of gas and huddled close. As her body shook, Greta imagined a finite number of tremors, each one bringing her a step closer to warm. It comforted her, the counting. Minutes passed. Greta's skin thawed, but her limbs stiffened to the shape of the chair. Rigor mortis. A battle clashed inside of her—stand up or run and hide. What was happening to Ash at this moment? Her insides shook while her body stiffened.

As she considered busing back—the wait unbearable—a shadow flickered past the living-room window. The door slid open, dragging against the entryway carpet. Greta turned her head. Her neck worked. Ash stood in the doorway for a moment, the afternoon sun glaring bright around his body. She didn't turn away. Something loosened in her muscles. His body whole, in one piece. "Ashwin."

He closed the door, kicked off his shoes and walked to the kitchen. A purple bruise swelled on one cheek. He turned off the dial on the stove, the hiss of gas falling silent and the flame disappearing. How long had it been on?

"You're okay," she breathed. "I left you."

He slumped against a nearby counter. "I'm glad you left."

"Dylan hit you?"

"Some other knuckle-dragging cretin on the basketball team."

"I left you. I'm sorry. I couldn't—"

"Greta, it's okay."

"What were you thinking, attacking him in front of the whole school?" Blood moved through her body again, shifting her forward in her chair.

"You feel bad for that guy?" Ash's voice rose.

"No, not him." Dylan hadn't asked her if she wanted to. She didn't get a choice. And when she *did* have a choice, he decided it was the wrong choice. Discarded her. What would've happened if she hadn't been able to get cell reception at the cabin? Hitchhiking home in the middle of the night, a flimsy jacket against the cold? A blaze lit in her center, waking her body. After humiliating her, they had put her in a position for more abuse.

"I don't feel bad for him," Greta said. She didn't fault Ash for beating him. Dissecting that moment, peeling away the terror for Ash as the entire student body roiled around him, something else remained. Justice. Satisfaction at seeing Dylan flinch in pain, knocked flat, weak in front of every person at West Edmonton High. She wouldn't apologize for the feeling, even if it meant she was a sociopath. Sorrynotsorry.

"I was really scared for you though," she said. "And you'll never walk safely in that school again."

"I was expelled. I can't go back."

That knocked the breath from her. Of course they expelled him. An unprovoked attack in front of five hundred witnesses. In vindicating her, he had also left her. She dropped her head. Alone again in those hallways.

For a minute they let the silence settle between them.

"Can you tell me what happened?" Ash asked. He only knew she hadn't said yes. Maybe he pictured roofies in her drink or some savage attack in the locker room.

She sighed, trying to choose her words. What to include? What to leave out? "There was a party at Matt's cabin back in November. I drank too much and..." She nodded, like that's all there was to say. Was she blowing this way out of proportion?

"And?"

"I blacked out." She shook her head, trying to rouse more memories from that moment. "When I woke up in the morning, Dylan told me we'd had sex." She stumbled over the last words. Weird to be talking to Ash about sex, consensual or not. It violated some too-much-information-from-your-sibling rule. "I don't remember anything about it." She left out feeling emotionally smashed from that moment forward, every nerve in her body misaligned.

Ash's jaw stiffened, clenched tight. A choppy breath left his body.

"Maybe I seemed into it," she said. "I don't know."

"Did you say yes?"

"I had shaved my legs, like maybe I thought something was going to happen."

"Did you say yes?"

"I'm pretty sure I didn't say anything at all. I had a hard time talking." She remembered struggling to form words, Priya bent beside her. Then nothing after.

"Then I don't care about your bloody legs," he snapped. Greta flinched at the phrase. "An absence of no isn't a yes, Greta."

She paused for a moment. "There's something...else... you should know." It wouldn't help him to hear it, but she needed to shake off the weight of the lies. Why had she felt responsible for carrying them? "That night you came to pick me up from the cabin, something else happened."

Ash waited, grim. "Okay?"

"Dylan wanted to...you know...again." *Just say the words.* "I—I couldn't. I said no."

Ash nodded, his expression controlled.

"He got really mad, thought I was accusing him of being a predator. He told Rachel and Matt to leave without me." She swallowed. It sounded even worse out loud. "And they did. They drove away and left me there."

Ash looked away, muscles twitching up his neck to his ears. "'Brave knight' and 'protector,' my ass." He ground a fist against the tears on his cheeks.

"It's not your fault, Ash."

"Look, you should probably talk to a counselor or someone about this. It might have to be someone other than me"—he choked out the words—"because right now I could kill that guy with my bare hands."

"I don't want to talk about it. I don't want to think about it. I just want to move on with my life."

"It will change you. It probably already has."

She didn't know how to answer. Had it changed her already? From A student to dropout. Creeping through the school halls as though hunted by a tiger. Alternating between self-loathing and confusion. A year ago—a lifetime ago—she was dealing with Patty and missing her mom. It was enough, even that. But this.

"Maybe you should go to the police," Ash said.

"No!" Reports, statements, probing exams, digging around the school. Cornering people for interviews. It would be her word against West Edmonton High royalty. Every nasty detail dragged out, examined, questioned. Or discounted and thrown away before it even started. A whole new world of humiliation. "And don't you dare. I'll never forgive you."

"It's your choice. I'll leave it up to you."

"Thank you."

He watched her, then filled his chest a few times before speaking. Trying to muster something, Greta thought.

"I'm sorry for freaking out," he finally said. "That won't help you, I know. You can talk to me, Greta."

She looked him in the face, saw a forced softness there. But his hands were rolled in tight fists, knuckles white. Veins popped at his wrists. An energy—a suppressed tremor—ran from his planted feet to his stiff neck. No, he couldn't be her counselor, her impartial listener, as she worked through this story again and again.

. . . .

Greta had sent Ash up first. She'd meant to follow behind him, after a few minutes to compose herself, but couldn't move from the sofa until hours after the sun had set. When did it start taking this much energy just to exist? She let herself in the door to Elgin's suite, the heat a relief as she stepped through. Not a single light on the upper floor. Just the streetlights through the uncovered windows.

Before starting down the hall to her bedroom, Greta glanced into the living room. She almost missed him this time, slumped lower than normal in his chair. The moonlight outlining his hair like a handful of feathers.

"Elgin?" she whispered. Had he fallen asleep?

"I'm here."

She settled into the chair beside him. Their spots now. "Ash and I had some things to sort out. We thought it was better not to do it in your space."

"About his expulsion?"

"He told you?" What else did he say?

"Yes. The school called. Your brother gave them my number. I guess I'm the closest thing to a guardian."

Greta sank lower in her chair. Elgin, who put a roof over their heads and served them home-cooked meals, now had to field angry phone calls from their principal. What more would they ask of him? "Did Ash tell you what happened?"

"A little. The principal told me he got in a fight. I guess Ash didn't care much for that boy."

Greta tried not to laugh. That was one way of putting it. "Sorry you had to deal with that."

"Oh, it's okay. It made me a nostalgic for Alice's school days." He chuckled. So Alice had been a little monster too.

Passing headlights on the street drew their eyes out the front window. Greta didn't want to think about when the sun would rise again. When Ash would stay and she would go. How would she finish school now? How would he?

"I'm sorry I didn't get any dinner made tonight," Elgin said. "Wasn't feeling up to it, to be honest."

"That's okay. You really don't have to."

"But I like to. It's just that"—he paused—"after Eleanor died, after the cancer, I haven't quite been myself. Alice says I suffer from depression." He said the word like a grade schooler reading from a medical textbook.

"And what do you say?"

She felt him move beside her. "I don't know if I feel the need to sum it up in a word. That feeling though..." He braced his hands against his knees to push himself upright. Leaving the sentence unfinished, he picked an empty mug off the table and started toward the kitchen. Then stopped. "It feels like a wall between me and everything else."

A wall. Maybe. "I think of it more as a maze," Greta said. She sensed his proximity but felt okay.

"Yes, a maze." He nodded, then slouched beside her. "It feels like standing in the middle of a maze. You wake up, no idea how you got there."

"There are paths all around you," Greta continued. "At least one of them right. You know you should pick, start down one, dive in. But they all look exactly the same, so you just turn in a circle, looking at them."

As she spoke, Elgin turned his body to face the television, then the picture window, the bookcase covered in plants, and finally Greta. He said, "You keep waiting to feel a pull, for something to become clear. But it doesn't. So you turn round and round in a circle." Then he shuffled off into the darkness, his footsteps sounding in the kitchen, then down the hall.

Greta stood, her eyes tracing the invisible circle Elgin had tread in the living room, and followed behind him. She knew those ivy-covered walls well.

THIRTEEN

Greta slept, exhaustion shutting down every cell in her body. In the early morning, when she rolled over and heard Ash's slow breathing, she woke like a flash of light. A door inside of her cracked open, and her brain jammed its foot in the space. She lay in the dark and followed one spidery thought to the next. They all led back to the same place: *How could she do it without Ash?*

Impossible to continue as before, now that Ash had beaten up Dylan in front of the whole school. If they didn't know it before, they'd know now that she was Ash's sister. She needed a truce, and it had to come from the top. Rachel? Dylan and Matt would never forgive Greta, but Rachel had a way of reining them in. Maybe she could advocate for Greta, quell the uprising. And Rachel had always seemed uncomfortable with the way things sat between them. Maybe a small opening still existed. They'd been friends once.

Greta pulled her phone toward the bed, tugging on the charger cord. She hid the bright screen under her blanket, shielding Ash, and texted, **Can we meet before school? Somewhere we can talk in private.** 4:46 AM. She waited.

Close to six thirty, as her body started to drift, the phone vibrated. Rachel. **OK. See you in the library at 8.**

When she told Ash, he wanted to go with her.

"You're not allowed back on school property," Greta said. "Don't make things worse."

"I don't care. I don't trust her. What if she brings those assholes with her?"

"What are they going to do to me in a library?" But she knew Rachel wouldn't bring Dylan or Matt. Sneaking off to see her was an act of treason—fraternizing with the enemy. She was surprised Rachel had agreed so easily.

"I've stopped imagining what they could do," Ash snorted. "They surpass my expectations every time."

"I have to try to make some kind of peace, Ash, or at least explain my side of the story. There's no way I can finish the school year like this."

He sighed. "Now I get why you never wanted to go before. Just promise me you won't put up with any crap."

"I won't."

"You could definitely take her, if it comes to that."

Greta smiled. "I could." She texted Nate, asking if they could leave twenty minutes early.

In the library, a few people milled around or sat at tables, books spread out in front of them. Greta wandered, running her fingers along the spines of paperbacks, scanning the blurbs on the back without comprehending the words.

She couldn't stand still, the door always in her view. Eight o'clock came and went. Greta checked her phone compulsively, Ash's paranoia whispering in her ear.

At 8:08, a shadow crossed Greta's hand as she reached for her phone again. Rachel. Greta glanced around the room, just in case. Only the two of them, standing by the romance paperbacks.

Rachel ducked her head and smiled, like old times. "Greta. I was surprised to hear from you. How are you?"

Greta didn't know how to answer. "I thought it was time we talked." She paused. "And I think I need your help."

Rachel pulled her over to a round table in the corner, far from anybody else. "What do you need my help with?"

Greta slid into a chair and waited for Rachel to do the same. She felt a pang, Rachel smiling at her like they shared a good secret. Like stepping into the sun after too long in the shade. She shoved away another memory—the one of Rachel's car peeling away on snow-covered gravel. "First of all, I want you to know I didn't ask Ash to beat up Dylan. I had no idea he'd do that."

The smile dropped from Rachel's mouth. "I didn't think so. Didn't really seem like you. What happened?"

"Well, I had a...realization, I guess. That night at the cabin"—it never got easier, saying these words—"I never said I wanted to sleep with Dylan." She cleared her throat. "It wasn't consensual. I finally told Ash."

Rachel smiled again, this time like a mother being told by her child that heffalumps and woozles actually exist.

"Greta"—she shook her head—"why are you saying this? Dylan was really upset when you accused him of that before."

Only then it wasn't an accusation. She'd only gotten as far as implying she hadn't exactly raced to his bed with cheerleader-level enthusiasm. And then she'd rejected him, which probably didn't happen a lot.

"I know it sounds stupid," Greta said, "but it's taken me a while to understand that I wasn't given a choice. He didn't ask me. I didn't say yes."

Rachel's smile drooped, irritation tightening her mouth. "Greta, I was there."

"Fill me in then." A sickening panic bloomed in her gut. What if Rachel was right, that she'd said yes, been more than willing, and was now playing the victim card?

"You were all over him that night," Rachel said.

"I remember some of that, yes. We kissed. I sat on his lap."

"Well, you can understand why Dylan thought you were game."

Greta sighed, trying to find words to make sense of it. "Here's the thing. I really liked him. I liked kissing him. I liked sitting on his lap." Then she stopped. Ever since she'd dropped that confession on Ash, on herself, she had started to unravel the I-made-a-mistake-and-regret-it story she'd fabricated in her mind. "But if I'm honest, I didn't plan on staying over that night. And I didn't plan on sleeping with him—at least, not then."

"So why did you?"

"This is what I'm trying to tell you!" Greta hissed, straining across the table. "I drank too much and wasn't given a choice." A girl wandered close, saw Rachel's and Greta's faces and beelined to a shelf on the other side of the library.

"If you wanted to leave, why'd you drink so much? You could've said something sooner."

"Well…" She knew Rachel wouldn't understand this. She'd never had to work to save face or impress anyone. "I didn't really know how to get out of it."

Rachel leaned back in her chair and crossed her arms. "So you're blaming Dylan instead? He was drunk too, you know."

"Rachel, I couldn't even speak."

"You'd been giving him the green light all night."

"Did you actually see or hear me say yes?"

"I wasn't exactly hanging out in your bedroom."

"But what about getting *to* the bedroom? How'd that happen?"

Rachel furrowed her brow and looked away. "Dylan kind of helped you up the stairs."

"So he could walk and I couldn't?"

Rachel sighed and raked her fingers along her scalp. "I can see where you're going with this, and I won't be a part of it. I don't get it, Greta." Her smile was long gone. She squinted across the table. "Are you really religious or something?"

Greta shook her head.

"Then just desperate for attention," Rachel said, pushing her chair back and standing. "Everyone has done things they regret, but it's wrong to blame someone else. I don't want to hear any more." She walked away, her hair swishing at her waist.

Greta's whole body fell out of alignment, wrong to her core. A mannequin hammered together with mismatched parts. She fought the urge to hurl a book at Rachel's retreating head. Retreating for the second time. Shame leaked from her bones again. *Drama queen. Liar.* She wrestled with the feeling and nearly convinced herself that Rachel was wrong.

Then she stood, staring vacantly at the other students in the library. It was busier now. Some people talked low in groups. A startling burst of laughter came from a few shelves over. Greta turned to face the door, which swung open and closed as bodies came and went. Out that door, up a flight of stairs, her social studies class would begin any minute, Angus pretending not to notice her as she slid into her seat. Or slut-shaming her for not choosing him. Dodging that tiger in the hallways between classes. Slouching with Nate behind the ficus tree. A target on her back for being Ash's sister.

She shifted to face the library window. Outside that window, Ash. Elgin. Alice. A warm home bursting with green leaves. Somewhere, her dad and Patty. The rest of the world. People going to work. Cars. Buses. Planes. A big, big sky. All of them teeming on an engorged anthill. She swayed in a circle between the library door and the window.

. · · · .

Greta found Ash in the living room, staring down at the crumpled form of Elgin on the sofa. Hard to tell his sallow skin from the folds of the blanket. He usually ensconced himself in his bedroom late morning. Today it looked like he had walked by the sofa and collapsed. A drive-by sleep attack.

If Ash felt surprised to see her, he didn't show it. "We broke him," he said, thrusting his chin toward Elgin.

"Shh." Greta elbowed Ash's arm. "He can still hear you." But she did lean closer to check for movement in his chest, the flicker of REM sleep behind his eyelids. "He's just sleeping."

Ash turned to look at her, his eyes wide. "Are you sure about that?" Greta steered him by the elbow to the kitchen. Before she could speak again, Ash said, "It's too much, all this cooking for us," he sputtered, "and dealing with our crap. We're killing the man."

"I'll call Alice," Greta said, "just in case." Elgin had written her number in Sharpie on the side of the fridge. Not even on a sticky note—actual Sharpie on the fridge surface. "And we'll do more. We'll do all the cooking." They already did most of the cleaning, except for any plant-related stuff. Elgin practically bodychecked them whenever they attempted to touch a plant.

Greta left a voice mail for Alice. They stood over Elgin for another minute before withdrawing to their room, leaving him to sleep. Greta flopped on the air mattress and Ash on his bed. Midmorning sun shone through the gauzy curtains. They lay on their backs, staring up at the popcorn ceiling.

"So how'd it go?" Ash asked, without turning his head.

Greta shook her head. "Not well."

Now Ash craned his neck to look at her. "Did she come alone?"

"Yes." Greta let it sit for a minute. "She just didn't believe me."

Ash nodded, like he wasn't surprised. "You came home. Now what?"

"Ash, can I just...have a day?" Greta said. He didn't respond. "I have no idea what happens next for either of us. I need a day, maybe even two."

Ash lay still. After a few minutes Greta wondered if he'd fallen asleep. She felt drowsy herself, heat pumping through the air vents and sunshine beaming through the window onto her skin. The first truly quiet moment in months. They had walked, run, driven, scrubbed, shouted, fought, shoveled, worried and cried. Today they lay on unmade beds in Elgin's guest room, uncomfortably warm for Edmonton in February. At that moment Greta refused to turn in circles in the maze. She wanted to sit in the shade of its walls and have no idea which direction to take. To not even care. For one day. She filled her lungs and belly with air and released it slowly, again and again.

"Ash?"

"Hmm."

"Can I see the three pictures?"

Silence. Then, "Are you sure?"

"Yes."

For some reason it was Ash's job to get them—they both knew it. He pushed himself off the bed and left the room. Greta heard him open the door to the staircase leading to the basement and waited a few minutes. A hornet in her belly buzzed with anger, anxiety, fear. The sun burned it away, though, and the feeling didn't pierce her.

Ash came back and set the shoebox on the dresser, brushing dust off the lid. He picked three photos right off the top of the pile and handed them to her hesitantly, as if they were the results of a cancer biopsy.

Greta's heart sank at the first photo—a version of what she had feared. Their mom sliding a lit birthday cake in front of her and Ash, only the back of her head and one cheek visible. Greta counted the candles: their fifth birthday. Ash, with a messy mop of hair, smiled like he'd been handed a pony. Greta in partial silhouette as well. Still, a good moment, one retained only by the picture. Greta couldn't recall anything about their fifth birthday.

A pang of joy and jealousy at the second one. Diana's and Ash's faces filled the whole photo. Roger—the invisible photographer—stood close. Diana's skin was washed pale from the flash. Greta noticed Diana's slightly crooked teeth, and Ash's new adult teeth, still too large for his mouth. What had happened to that look, a lightness—even joy—in his eyes? Was it snuffed out at once when Diana died? Slowly siphoned from him over The Patty Years? A natural part of growing up?

A passerby must have taken the third photo, all of them together at Hawrelak Park. Roger and Diana stood with their arms around each other's waists, smiling for the camera. Roger, an inch shorter than his wife, had a lot more hair than now. Greta leaned her head against her mother, and Ash, on Roger's side, clutched a bread bag and watched a nearby goose. This was before they knew bread wasn't good for geese or ducks. It had always galled Roger, years later, when posted signs made other suggestions: halved grapes, grain. "The ducks eat better than we do," he complained.

Greta propped all three pictures against a stack of textbooks on the dresser. "We'll have to get some frames."

Ash got up from the bed and stood beside her. He overlapped two photos, blocking out Roger completely.

"He's still your father, Ash," Greta said.

Ash shook his head. "He's not. He chose that."

She didn't want to get into it with him, didn't even know if he was wrong. Maybe she was the human carpet, and he was the sensible one. Greta didn't mind that photo—the Before Family. If Patty had been resting her pruny little chin on Roger's shoulder, Greta would have hidden that part too. Cut it off.

FOURTEEN

Greta intended to chip the ice off the porch and scrub the bathtub, but her body wanted to collapse every time she stood. Ash watched her, frowning, when she got up off the air mattress and flopped back down within five seconds. "What's wrong?" he asked.

"I'm just feeling tired." Three months of tired all at once. Maybe even seven years of tired—all the energy needed to balance on the bucking surface of life with Patty. Plus the two years of fog after their mother died. And the death itself. Nine-years tired, in every cell and organ in her body.

"Just take it easy then. I'll do the work," Ash said, his mouth poised to ask more.

She settled with a book near Elgin, watching to see that he shifted and murmured in his sleep. Still alive, just tired too. Something about Elgin calmed her. Even as he stood on the edge of his own personal precipice, Greta knew he would never drag them off with him.

Alice arrived before supper, slipping through the front door without knocking. Ash was frying chicken for quesadillas, while Greta was curled up in the chair near Elgin, her book fallen to the side. She sat up as Alice approached.

"He's been there, sleeping, all day," Greta said, standing next to Alice. She swayed as the weight of her body dropped to her limbs. "Think something's wrong?"

"Well, whatever it is, it's always wrong," Alice said, looking over Elgin's sleeping form. "He goes through something like this every January and February."

"Is that when your mom died?" Greta asked.

"No. It's just when he loses all hope."

February. A test of endurance. How did any of them survive? Greta nodded. She felt it too—each day rewound to the beginning and repeated itself. The longest short month of the year.

"Dad." Alice leaned over and rubbed his head like a lucky penny. "Dad." Her hand rested on his cheek for a moment. Greta startled at the tender gesture.

Elgin opened his eyes and smiled at Alice, stretching his body long before deflating again. "I didn't know you were coming." He blinked, sleepy.

"Well, your roommates here were concerned you were dying."

Elgin still smiled at Alice. She could say anything, really—*I've come to mutilate you*—and he would smile. "Just tired lately. I'm not sleeping at night."

"Want me to make an appointment with your doctor?"

"No, no." He waved his hand at her, shooing her away. "I'll be fine."

Greta suspected Elgin's definition of *fine* differed from the rest of the world's.

Alice and Greta helped Ash in the kitchen while Elgin watched the setting sun out the front window. Snow dunes and front lawns disturbed by boot prints and the odd spray of dog urine.

"Ash and I are worried we're putting extra stress on your dad by being here," Greta said, leaning in close to Alice. Ash put down the cheese grater and stood on Alice's other side.

"No," Alice said, looking back and forth between them. "In fact, you may have delayed the worst of it by being here, if I'm honest. It probably helped him to have someone to look after again."

Greta's chest loosened a bit. She couldn't stand the thought of her and Ash as tiny parasites, gnawing away at Elgin. "Why don't you live here with him?" she asked Alice. "You're in school. You could even stay in the basement and save him having to get renters." The rent money went to her anyway. Dealing with Patty probably hadn't helped his mental health.

"No way." Alice held her hands up, motioning for them to stop right there.

"Why not?" Ash asked.

"I cannot deal with...*that*...every day." She looked toward the living room, Elgin's head silhouetted against the picture window.

"*That?* Ouch," Ash said.

"Look," Alice said, "I know this sounds cold, but I cannot deal with all his stuff on a daily basis. Whether he lives or dies, even," Alice continued, "can't come down to me. Don't ask me to be responsible. It's not fair. Could you fix your mother's cancer?"

Both Ash and Greta looked down at the counter, studying the diced tomatoes in front of them. This level of honesty didn't sit in a nice compartment. Alice's words rang true to Greta—harsh out loud, but true. At the same time, how often did the presence of Ash, doing nothing but existing, buoy her up?

"I hear you," Greta said. "I really do. What if you came a little more often?"

"Not just once a month to collect his money," Ash added.

Alice wagged a finger at him. "Don't even." All the honesty cards were on the table now. To Greta, she said, "I'll think about it. I've worked hard to get some distance from him and create stability in my own life. I guess I always felt I had to keep him at arm's length."

"He's definitely bat-shit crazy," Ash said. Only Greta blinked at that. "But he's a good man. I envy you, to tell the truth."

Alice's head snapped to look at him, but he'd already turned back to the chicken on the stove.

Bat-shit crazy. Funny. Lately Elgin was the only one who made sense to Greta.

Elgin waved away their offers of food. While Ash and Greta cleaned the kitchen, Alice took him a plate and sat in

Greta's chair, coaxing him to eat a little. Greta thought she heard a few threats as well.

When Greta collapsed in a kitchen chair, her body heavy again, both Alice and Ash joined her. Ash produced a deck of cards from somewhere, flipping one card back and forth between his fingers, trying to master a trick.

"You guys graduate this spring?" Alice asked.

Ash and Greta looked at each other. "I got expelled," Ash said, the card bending under the weight of his fingers.

Alice snorted. "What'd you do?"

"Beat up this guy…in front of the whole school…during a pep rally."

Alice practically beamed. "No! That was on my bucket list!"

Greta nodded, grim. "He did."

"Was he a jerk or something?" Alice asked.

"The biggest." Ash's eyes wandered to Greta and back down to the cards again. Alice didn't miss the gesture and subdued her glee, glancing at Greta for a nanosecond.

"Well"—Alice cleared her throat—"I'm sure he deserved it." Greta was grateful she didn't ask for details or what they were going to do next. "And I have a confession too."

Ash and Greta waited.

"I'm getting a tattoo."

"What and where?" Greta asked.

"Right here." Alice pushed up her sleeve and rubbed a spot on her upper arm. "A Celtic symbol for strength."

"What does that look like?" Ash asked.

"Here." She grabbed his arm and started tracing curving lines on his skin with her finger. "Actually, do you mind if I use a pen?"

Ash shook his head, still watching the place where Alice had drawn the invisible symbol. She came back with a Sharpie—Elgin's Sharpie—and uncapped it. Gripping Ash's arm with her left hand, she drew the curved, intersecting lines with her right. Her brow furrowed, and long hair fell onto his bare arm and wrist. Greta watched Ash's eyes leave the symbol and examine Alice's face, close to his. Greta felt like an intruder, watching them. Then Alice pulled back and put the lid on the Sharpie, triumphant.

Ash lifted his arm to examine the symbol. "It's nice. It'll look good." He noticed Greta now and cleared his throat, shifting away from Alice.

Alice swung her purse off the back of the chair. "I'm going out for a smoke."

"I'll go with you," Ash said, prompting Greta to give him a classic Ash-style eyebrow raise. He might have recognized it had he looked her way. They slipped out the front door and settled on the top step of the porch. Through the screen door, Greta watched Alice light the cigarette and smile as she blew a stream of smoke above their heads. After a minute she offered it to Ash, who took a drag in a way that told Greta he'd done it a hundred times before. She felt a pang, watching him. What secret parts of his life did he shield from her?

Elgin sighed, possibly about the cloud of smoke drifting through his sunset. Greta got up and stood behind him.

"We dug out some old pictures today," she told him. Was it wrong, burdening him with another dead person? "Want to see what my mom looked like?"

"Of course."

Greta pulled the photos off the dresser, her touch gentle. She settled next to Elgin and showed him the photos in the same order she'd seen them. Elgin blinked, sat a little straighter and looked back and forth between Diana's and Greta's faces. "You're certainly your mother's daughter."

Greta smiled and rubbed away a fingerprint on the corner of the picture. "This was about two years before she was diagnosed with cancer. She looks happy, doesn't she?"

Elgin nodded. "She does."

Outside on the porch, Ash smiled too—possibly even matching the we-get-bacon smile—at something Alice said.

"The thing is"—Greta hesitated—"I wish I could remember her like this."

"You don't? Too young?"

"I can't seem to get past the time when she was sick. I don't remember much from before, and every time I think of her, I remember how she suffered. I hardly recognized her." She swallowed.

"There are only two times in my life I have felt the distance pain puts between people," Elgin said. "One was when Eleanor was in labor with Alice. I was with her, trying to help, but she only had one foot in our world until it was over." He paused before saying more. "The other was near the end of the cancer." Elgin always called it "the cancer," like there was only one. *The cancer to end all cancers.* He paused again, the words sucking his energy. "The human body, how it fails you in the end."

That was the thing about being with Elgin. He said everything perfectly—you didn't have to speak at all.

. · · ·.

That night, trying to sleep on an air mattress with a possible leak, Greta thought of something. She unplugged her phone from its charger and stood, wobbling on the flattening mattress. Ash had propped the photos in a line on the dresser like before, with Roger covered. Turning on the flashlight app, Greta shone the light across each photo. Her mom wore a flowery green blouse on their birthday, a lime-green tank top with Ash and a forest-green T-shirt (maybe Roger's?) at Hawrelak Park.

What was Mom's favorite color? Greta texted. Pressed *Send*.

Less than thirty seconds later, the message symbol lit up Greta's phone. Roger. **Green**, he answered.

FIFTEEN

The knock came from far away. It fit into Greta's dream about a man hammering a boat. Then she bolted up on her elbows, rolled off the mattress and shuffled to the door. Something urgent about knocking. *Make the noise stop.*

Nate, standing in flurries. "Hey." Snowflakes clung to his eyebrows—a ginger Yeti. "Are you coming?" He eyed her rumpled shorts and sweaty T-shirt. The cold air shriveled her lungs and dry throat. Every night at Elgin's felt like some kind of sweat-detox program.

"No, I'm…"—she didn't know what to say—"…not."

Nate waited, holding his backpack in one hand and car key in the other. "Ever again?" His shoulders dropped, like the key suddenly weighed a lot.

The words sounded so definitive, but it was hard to imagine that one morning she would wake up and suddenly want to go back. The thought stirred a swirl of anxiety in her chest, an eddy in her gut. "I don't know what I'm doing, Nate. And you know Ash can't go back."

He waited for her to say more, snow the size of corn-flakes clinging to his wayward strands of hair. He thought for a minute, then said, "You two should sleep over at my house tonight."

"Uh..." She was eight years old again, standing in the schoolyard.

"Tomorrow's Saturday. It's not a school night." Still eight years old.

"I'll ask"—Greta actually started to say *Elgin*—"Ash."

Nate gave a nod and backed off the porch, leaving prints in the gauzy layer on the steps. "I'll call later." Before shutting the front door, Greta watched him lope over to Rebus and climb inside.

She had stayed up late, cradling her phone, fingers poised over the keypad. A battle waged. Her first impulse was to text Roger back as quickly as possible. Rapid-fire questions: *Where are you? Why did you leave? What are you doing? When are you coming back?* Also, confessions to share, one autocorrect word at a time: *We couldn't find jobs. Had to move upstairs with the landlord. Ash got expelled. Currently both dropouts.*

She stopped herself each time, sometimes getting a word or two down before deleting them. She couldn't win this one. If she texted again and he didn't answer, she'd be mad as hell. If he texted back and said he was hanging out with Patty in some dive, mad as hell. If he apologized for living like a frat boy instead of a middle-aged father, mad as hell. Though silence would be the worst. She couldn't risk it, that wound. She knew—and knew Roger knew—the **Green** text didn't really exist. A gift not to be acknowledged. A wink between corrupt politicians. She couldn't even tell Ash. He'd blow it up twenty different ways.

Greta bent to drink from the bathroom tap before slipping back inside the bedroom. Ash starfish-sprawled on top of his blanket, undisturbed by the scene at the door. She climbed into bed, not ready to be awake in the quiet house by herself. She thought about sleepovers when they were kids. Ash used to love the idea of a sleepover until it was actually time to go. Then he would cling to Diana or Roger. Diana would cajole him, whisper in his ear, "Go enjoy yourself! Home will always be here!"

Greta shook her younger self, shouted a message back through time: *Run, run home. Hold on tight. It will disappear.* What remained? Ash. Two children clinging to a buoy in the middle of an ocean storm.

The phone pinged. *Roger.* She scrambled for it, accidentally bumping it to the floor with a clatter. Ash smacked his lips and rolled on his side.

A new number. Not Roger, Rachel or Nate. **Its been a few days. Whats going on?** Greta stared at the two sentences. A few days since what? School? Someone who'd noticed she'd been gone but didn't know anything else.

Who is this? Greta texted back.

A pause. **Priya.**

Priya? Really? Greta didn't know what to tell her. What *was* going on? And how much did she want to share with Priya? **Not much**, Greta answered.

R u coming back to school?

Idk. She sent it and waited a full minute for a reply.

Can we meet?

This time Greta waited before responding. What did Priya want? If she'd told Greta the truth before, that she wasn't exactly the president of the Rachel and Dylan Fan Club, maybe she wanted a trash-talk session. Or was this about reconciliation with that group? **Why?** Greta texted back.

Just want to talk to u. No more than half an hour. Meet at Mulligans at lunchtime?

Just the two of us?

Yes.

Ash wouldn't like it. A sniper drawing her out alone to get a good shot. She could invite him along—not on school property, after all—but what kind of conversation would they have with him glowering nearby? **OK. I'll come.** Curiosity egged her on. Priya wouldn't hurt her, would she? Unintentionally make her feel inadequate—yes. Actually inflict pain—no.

Greta watched the room lighten. Ash rolled onto his side, the pink crescent scar visible on his bare back. She tried playing a game on her phone with the sound off but then set it aside, annoyed by the tedious blinking lights. She couldn't sit here all morning, waiting for an argument with Ash.

Can you meet sooner? Greta texted Priya and waited. This mystery meeting made her twitchy. Plus, to make Ash happy, a last-minute change might throw off Priya's plans to drag someone along.

One minute passed. Two minutes. Then: **You mean right now?**

In about half an hour.

Greta knew Priya was probably in the middle of a class. The phone screen slipped into sleep mode, waiting. A minute later it brightened with a message. **See you in half an hour.**

This had better not be a repeat of her meeting with Rachel, where she'd basically said, "You're an attention-hungry prude who preys on innocent jocks." Greta stood on shaky footing—a homemade rope bridge dangling over a ravine—but held fast to the one fact: *I didn't say yes.* Then clarity got lost in the details. She always returned from that memory with a blank feeling of loss. She didn't need someone kicking more dirt on it.

Greta threw on the previous day's clothes and ran a brush through her hair. As Ash stirred in bed, she slipped out the front door and jogged two blocks to catch a bus. Sun glared off the snow, making water prick her eyes. Her parka hung open, cooling her flushed body.

Mulligans was three blocks from the school, the kind of place that made grilled-cheese sandwiches and called them "panini" or served Sprite from a can as "limonata." Priya sat in a booth near the window. For some reason, Greta had wanted to get there first, to anchor herself in a spot before Priya showed up.

"Hey." Greta slipped into the vinyl seat across from Priya, suddenly breathless.

"Hi, Greta." Priya paused between words, like she had to think about Greta's name. Then she smiled, as if waiting for Greta to speak first. Her arms thin in a black sweater, cat eyeliner.

"How are you?" Greta started with that. The only thing she really knew to say.

"Good. Not bad." Priya nodded, looking around them. Only a few others—a group in their midtwenties—sat on stools at the bar, drinking coffee. "You?"

Greta gave the same kind of nod, tapping her fingers on the tabletop. The server came over. Greta ordered a limonata, and Priya asked for a cappuccino.

After the server left, Priya looked at Greta and steepled her fingers. She said, "So I noticed you haven't been around since the…incident…in the gym."

Greta sighed and looked away. Too much to say about that. "Nope. I'm sure you can understand why."

"Wow, that was…something." Priya started to chuckle and then pulled it in, like it had slipped out unintentionally. "I wouldn't want to be on your brother's bad side." Greta didn't want to tell her she already was—lumped in with the rest of them.

"I didn't ask him to beat up Dylan." She felt defensive for Ash, her ferocious ally. "I was just as surprised as everyone else."

"Oh"—Priya snorted—"I'm sure Dylan had it coming. It's just that no one else in that school has the balls." She laughed again, this time unapologetically.

The server plunked the drinks on the table and walked away, probably sensing an abysmal tip. Greta knew she wouldn't be back.

"So why did you want to see me?" Greta needed to know the trajectory of this, what to steel herself for.

Priya stopped and cleared her throat. "Okay. I know you didn't have the best experiences with my friends, and then your brother beat up Dylan. But"—she drew out the word—"I don't think it's fair for you to be chased away from school."

When Greta didn't answer, Priya continued. "Look, I know we haven't exactly been close, but I can't help but feel something's not right here." She looked at Greta, almost shy. "That maybe you're paying for something you didn't do."

She knew. At least part of it. The way she leaned forward and peered into Greta's eyes, trying to prop open a stubborn gate and hold it there.

Greta looked to the people at the bar, smiling, chatting so easily. "You talked to Rachel?"

Priya nodded without looking away. "She finally told me their side of things. They're all pissed about it. I don't think anyone else knows."

"What I said was true." Anger coated each of her words.

Priya nodded. "Can you tell me your side?"

Greta studied Priya's face. To trust her or not? Part of Greta clamored to tell her side, could hardly hold the words back. *I'm here! I've been cut off and made to disappear. I'm here!* The other part restrained her, held everything tight, protected. Goddess Priya—did she bring blessing or wrath? That was always the question. But Greta wasn't at West Edmonton High anymore. Why did she still protect them? Protect them to protect herself?

"This is my side," Greta said, sitting up straight. "I was too drunk to walk or talk that night at the cabin, and then Dylan told me the next morning that we'd had sex. For a while I just thought I'd made a mistake—used bad judgment—but then I realized I hadn't had the chance to say yes or no. I finally told Ash, and you saw what happened next."

A flicker of something in Priya's eyes, and her face tightened. Greta wanted to snatch back her words, regretting her trust. She folded her arms to protect her center, the smashed pieces of her insides waking to pinch her again.

"I felt a little worried leaving you there," Priya said, looking down. "I should have stayed or brought you with me."

Guilt. The goddess Priya felt guilty. "I don't blame you, Priya. You tried." She left out the part about not wanting to leave with Priya, that stupid jealousy that seemed now like a spat over a Ken doll. "That's the last thing I remember, actually."

Priya's face twitched. She pulled her body up to match Greta's, somehow seeming taller than her. "I believe you, Greta."

The words reached Greta, stilling her insides. Blood, bones, flesh grew and bloomed. The Greta who stood alone against the whole school threw back her shoulders and drew her first real breath. Of course Ash believed her too. But he would stand by her side and fight like a badger no matter what she told him, take on anyone he felt had wronged her.

Greta cleared her throat, fighting the urge to leap from her seat and bear-hug Priya. "Thank you." Not enough. Not nearly enough. She exhaled a slow breath to steady herself. "That means a lot to me."

"Well," Priya said, "I know Dylan. He isn't one to ask permission. I remember when we were dating, he used to take my hands and put them...on him." Priya looked away, like she'd said too much. "That was a red flag for me. I knew it wasn't going to work out."

"Did they tell you about the weekend after that?" Greta asked.

"No." Priya shook her head, frowning. "There's more?"

Greta told her about refusing Dylan, his meltdown and being left behind. Ash having to steal Patty's car to rescue her. She left out the panic. That awful panic, wandering in the dark, fear hovering like a pack of ghouls. Shame. Embarrassment. Fear. Even now, they lingered close.

Priya flopped back in her seat, her mouth falling open. "*What?*"

Greta nodded, nothing more to say.

After a moment of gasping, Priya said, "I can't believe it. I mean, I can, but I can't." She shook her head, trying to make sense of the words. "I *can* believe that Dylan thinks every human on the planet wants to sleep with him. It must've hurt his tender little feelings when you said no. So he left you to die in the woods?" She swore. "And Rachel and Matt went along with it." Her cheeks flushed red and her arms twitched, as if the anger was attacking her body.

"Here's the thing I can't shake," Greta said. It was a leap, a mighty leap off the side of a building. But she had to say it, while Priya still whirled off-kilter. "I can't help but feel I was responsible for some of this. Not all of it, but like I played a part."

Priya recoiled. "Say what?" When Greta didn't answer immediately, she asked, "What part might that be?"

"Well, for one, I drank way too much. I was trying to keep up with everyone, and I hardly drink at all. That was stupid."

"Greta—"

"It wouldn't have happened if I'd been sober, or at least not passed out." There it was. Greta realized the weight of those words as soon as she hoisted them onto Priya. So many layers to work through. So many stories she had whispered to herself.

"Greta." Priya reached across the table and touched Greta's hand. "I've drunk too much at parties before too. Guess what happened to me?"

"You got sick?"

"Yeah, I did. I've thrown up. Once, I passed out. I've had hangovers."

Greta waited for her to continue.

"This kid at my old school got alcohol poisoning. That was kind of scary. But those are some of the things that happen to your body when you drink too much. Guess what's not on that list?"

Greta shrugged.

"Getting raped."

Greta flinched. It was too much, that word. She wanted to protest. Priya had it wrong—full-on rape was something different. This was something different. But the words swelled and jammed in her throat. They pushed water into her eyes.

She rubbed it away, shielded by the heels of her hands, her protest still blocked inside of her.

"Anything else?" Priya asked, her voice gentle.

Greta nodded and took a drink of lukewarm fake limonata, trying to clear a way for more words. "I always felt stupid for saying no to Dylan the second time, when I'd already slept with him before." She heard the words outside her mouth, how absurd they sounded. But she'd gone this far. "Like, in a way I triggered what happened after."

"Well, Greta," Priya said, "you didn't consent to sleeping with him the first time. Also, what are you, a blow-up doll? You could've said yes a hundred times and still had a right to say no the hundred and first."

Greta nodded, her voice gone again. On one level she had already known it, everything Priya said. But hearing it out loud, from another person, freed her. This load she had carried with her, tried to sort through, rejected, then always picked up again—she could finally stand on the precipice and hurl it off the edge. She watched the rocks and boulders shrink to pebbles as they fell, then disappeared. Maybe gone for good.

Greta wanted to thank Priya again but was tired of that word—so useless and bland. Feelings like what she had right now should come with a gift-wrapped box of puppies and a mariachi band. *Here, Priya. This is how I feel. This.*

Priya smiled and touched Greta's hand again, squeezing it tightly. "Greta, I'm your woman on the inside now. What do you want me to do?"

Greta shrugged, not quite ready to speak and also not knowing what to say. She cleared her throat and took another drink. "Maybe just stick up for me if people talk about it."

"Yes, yes. Done. But what else?"

Greta shrugged again. What else could there be—a torture session in the foods lab? "That's all."

"Greta, Greta, Greta." Priya chuckled low. "You really are as kind as I suspected. You'd better leave the evil up to me. Too bad I don't have your brother at my disposal," she mused. "And when are you coming back to school?"

Greta gaped. After everything she'd just spilled, Priya had asked her when she was going back *there*. "I'm not going back. Not this term anyway."

"And let them win?" Priya's voice squeaked.

"It's not a battle, and I'm not some social-justice warrior. I'm just a person…"

Priya raised her eyebrows, waiting for Greta to finish.

"I'm just a person who feels a little less human every time I walk through those doors. Every minute of the day, I wonder when I'm going to win the humiliation lottery."

"But they're wrong, and you're right!"

"Yes, I know." And she really felt it now, after talking to Priya—it wasn't just some theory floating out there somewhere. "But the cost is too high for my…my soul, my humanness."

She expected Priya to make retching sounds after that explanation, but it was the best she could do. Pieces taken from her that she couldn't get back or that she fought to gather from diverse places and tried to reform, grotesque and misshapen. "I can't fight that battle right now." She felt, too, now that the weight had slid away, the sadness and anger— the wound that would need tending. Too much debris there before.

"Okay." Priya sighed, tapping her fingers on the table. "Okay. I don't know if I agree or fully understand, but I can respect that."

When they stood to leave, Greta stooped to hug her. Priya, small inside Greta's frame but strong. And surprisingly warm.

SIXTEEN

Greta arrived home to find Ash tearing up the house like someone who had lost the remote during the Stanley Cup playoffs. She closed the front door behind her and stared. Ash glanced up at the sound and straightened when he saw her.

"What are you doing?" she asked.

"Looking for you," he said, his shoulders squared defensively.

"Under a cushion?"

"I thought you might have left a note or something."

"Oh." Right. A note. She'd been gone a couple of hours, including the bus ride. "Sorry about that."

"I thought maybe you'd gone to school after all."

"Well, kind of," she said. Ash raised his eyebrows in a question. "I went to meet Priya."

"Why?" He looked distressed. "Why do you keep meeting with them?"

"She texted me, and we met in a very public place. She just wanted to talk." When he didn't look convinced, she added, "It went well. I think I have an ally now."

Watching her, Ash's face relaxed. "Good. I'm glad you could talk to her." He cleared his throat and didn't seem to know where to put his hands. They settled on his hips. Greta told him about Nate's sleepover invitation.

"Why? We live right across the street. Why do we need to sleep there?"

"Because he's our friend—our only friend—and he asked. I think he's worried about us," she added. Was Priya her friend now too?

"Yeah. Okay." She knew Ash couldn't deny they owed Nate big-time.

That evening they made tuna sandwiches and salad, leaving some in the fridge for Elgin and a note on the table. He shuffled out of his bedroom as they hauled pillows and blankets to the door.

"Moving out?" The alarm on Elgin's face matched his disheveled hair and puffy eyes.

"Sleeping at Nate's tonight," Greta said. "He invited us." She felt the need to smooth his hackles, that unstable worry. He didn't want them to move out?

"Sandwiches in the fridge," Ash said, pointing with his chin because of his full hands.

"Well, enjoy yourselves," Elgin said. "And your friend Nate can come here sometime too." He examined the over-watered fern on the table.

They tromped across the street to Nate's house, Greta dropping her pillow in a snowbank on the way. Nate swung the front door open before they knocked. He had made plans.

And written them on a small whiteboard hanging on the kitchen wall.

"My dad's out with friends until after midnight," Nate said, "so we'll have the place to ourselves." For most people their age, this would mean sneaking beer out of the fridge and an impromptu party in the basement. For Nate, it looked like...

"*Fondu*," Greta read from the top of the whiteboard list.

"One cheese, one chocolate," Nate said, banging around the kitchen. "I hope you didn't eat already."

"No." They lied in unison and helped him chop fruit at the counter.

When it was ready, they moved to the living room, which was decorated in various shades of beige. While they ate at the coffee table, leaning over each other with skewers, dribbling, they moved to whiteboard plan number two: watching the 1992 *Blade Runner*, director's cut. Ash shushed Greta every time she asked him to pass something, his fingers dragging in sauces as he grabbed random things and thrust them in her direction.

Number three: Scrabble. Greta knew Ash detested board games, with their cheerful colored cards and inconsequential points systems. Still, he didn't complain as Nate started clearing off the coffee table to set up the game.

"I'm going to win," Greta said.

"She's going to win," Ash echoed.

From the corner of the coffee table, Nate picked up a framed picture of a woman with flame-red hair and a crooked smile. He pressed it to his chest—an unconscious routine gesture. Then he jolted back to the present, eyes flitting between them, and placed it roughly on a nearby shelf. He didn't look at them, his hands reaching for dirty plates and spilled fruit.

"Is that your mom?" Greta asked. If she'd been truly kind, she'd have said nothing. He'd never mentioned her before, and they'd never seen her come or go. Divorced? Dead too?

"Yeah, that's her." His face flushed, knowing he'd been caught.

"Are your parents divorced?" Nate would have mentioned if she'd died, right?

"No, they're still married." He stopped moving, probably knowing he'd have to explain now.

Ash and Greta leaned forward, waiting.

"My mom's in the military, deployed in the Ukraine. She's an infantry officer, gone for six months at a time."

That wasn't on the list of anything Greta expected. She didn't know what to say. How terrible? How wonderful? Still alive, still married to Nate's father and could, at any moment, stand too close to a land mine. No wonder Nate cradled her picture and probably wished on falling stars. Nate, too, waiting, waiting for results. Either an embrace at the end of a long flight home or...

"That must be stressful," is what she said.

"I worry about her all the time." Nate crouched to unfold the game board.

"Why didn't you say something before?" Ash asked.

Nate shrugged, his the only pair of hands moving, turning over tiny letter tiles. "It seemed like you guys had enough to worry about." They didn't join in his busyness.

Ash and Greta shared a look. They had failed him—again. With Nate, always taking more than they gave. "Sorry if we made you feel that way," Greta said. Did they ever ask him about his life? She wracked her brain to remember a question, a conversation. Across from her, Ash dropped his head.

"You can talk to us about anything," she said, and Ash nodded, joining Nate in organizing the tiles.

"Okay," Nate said. "Okay then. I do have a question."

They looked up, waiting.

"How do you plan on finishing school and graduating?"

Neither of them answered. Ash started choosing his tiles, until Nate grabbed his and Greta's hands, forcing them to look at him.

"How do you plan on finishing school and graduating?" he asked again.

Ash wormed his hand away. "I don't know. They kicked me out, remember?"

"And you?" Nate turned to Greta.

Greta tried to quash a burst of irritation. "There's more to this story than you know," she said, trying to keep her voice even. But she couldn't lose it on Nate—practically the Mother Teresa of teenage boys. "I won't go back without Ash."

"Listen, I'm not saying you should go back because I don't have other friends there—I don't, but I'll be okay. As your friend, I'm telling you this is important."

"Dude, it's not an option," Ash said, in the same tone he'd used when Roger and Patty got on his back.

"And that's the only school in the city?" Nate asked. Greta had never seen him this tenacious before.

"Well, no…" she and Ash both mumbled.

"So how are you going to do it?"

"I don't know!" Greta snapped.

They all paused, eyeing each other. The old Nate seemed to return to his body, his voice less like a police interrogation. "I know I'm being pushy," he said, "but it's all still possible at this point. You've only missed a few days. If you miss a month, it's a different story. Promise me you'll try."

They looked at each other and then back at Nate. "We promise." A bit of a dark horse, their Nate.

Greta stood next to him later that night, holding her toothbrush as they lingered outside the bathroom and waited for Ash to finish.

"I'm sorry we've left you alone at that school," Greta said. "I know it's tough there."

Nate let out a puff of air. "To be honest, it wouldn't matter which school I'm at. I've tried, but I just don't fit in. Don't even know how. I would if I could." And what a disappointment that would be, a less-shiny version of Nate.

"Well, you've got us." She bumped his shoulder, making him sway.

"Thank you." He smiled down on her. "I get it, by the way, why you don't want to go back."

"Yeah?" Her gut tightened for a second. Would it be okay if Nate knew?

"It's a twin thing, right?" Nate said. "Some unspoken bond? One feels incomplete without the other?"

Greta laughed. He wasn't entirely wrong, just missing a few details. She leaned against his arm. Only a slight wobble. Almost as good as Ash.

She fell asleep on a foam mattress on the floor, with Ash and Nate playing Wizard's Quest at the coffee table, Ash complaining about the rules. Then jerked awake. Every light off. Silence. A shadow over her, bending closer. Greta gasped and scrambled back, bumping her head on the bookshelf.

"Greta, it's me." A whisper.

She held her hands out to push him away and pinched her eyes shut. Waiting for the weight of his body to crush her. Her heart filled her whole throat—she couldn't make a sound.

"I'm just bringing you an extra blanket."

She knew the voice. Nate. Another part of her brain registered a soft, feathery layer spread over her body. The shadow stepped away.

She dropped her hands and sucked in a breath. "Nate?" she yelped. Her back still pressed against the bookshelf, the only light from the moon through the window.

"Sorry if I woke you. It gets cold in here at night. I have extra blankets for you and Ash." He walked over to Ash's sleeping form on the sofa and draped one over him too. Ash didn't stir.

Greta drew another breath, aware of her sweat against the cold air. She watched Nate crawl into his own bed—a sleeping bag and crocheted pillow on the other side of the room. They didn't speak again.

Greta's heart dropped back down into her chest, still rattled. She focused on breathing, as though she'd been deprived for minutes and had to make up for it. Inching back under her blankets, Greta arranged the pillow under her head.

She thought Nate had gone to sleep when he asked her, "Were you having a bad dream or something?"

Greta swallowed, her throat dry. "Yeah. A bad dream."

. . . .

Greta saw it on her phone first, the inconspicuous white letters spelling out the date. She scrambled from her bed on the floor, the blankets tugging her legs like a giant finger trap. Ash, on the sofa, sat up and watched her.

"What's wrong?" he asked.

"Nothing's wrong," she whispered back, checking to see if Nate was still asleep. The curve of his spine faced them, unmoving. She gathered her clothes to get changed in the bathroom.

"Are you going to meet someone?"

Greta tried not to laugh. Who could she possibly meet up with next? Dylan? Matt? "No. I need to get something for Elgin. Don't worry about it."

Ash frowned. "Want me to come?"

"No, no." She waved for him to stay. "I'll be back soon." She scooted to the bathroom before he could say more.

. . ˙ ˙ .

They both arrived at Elgin's an hour later. Ash eyed her full arms and helped her shift things onto the table.

"Was this really necessary?" he asked.

"Shush."

"How much did it cost?" Alice had left them a hundred dollars after cashing the check from Roger.

"It doesn't matter." She would have easily dropped twice as much.

Then she hovered, her eye on Elgin's closed door. Didn't the man ever have to use the bathroom? She moved all his plants, dusted and put them back. Out of boredom, she made pancakes from scratch and pressured Ash into eating at least four of them.

Near noon, a creak in the hallway brought her running, socks sliding on the floor. Elgin, more wrinkle than man, stepped toward the bathroom door.

"Elgin." She grabbed his elbow, making him jump, and felt a pang of guilt at possibly triggering a heart attack. "Elgin, come see."

She dragged him down the hall, his skin papery under her fingers. Shoving him near the table, she stopped behind him and pointed over his shoulder.

He stared blankly at the green leaves, the curve of colored petals, the plastic cellophane shucked aside. "What's this?" he said, sounding a little more awake now.

"These are daffodils, and azaleas, and a tea rose plant." She stepped around him to point, in case her explanation wasn't clear. She'd taken the bus to Bunches, still too early in the year for the greenhouses that would spring up in grocery-store parking lots. "They're to plant in your garden later. Maybe in the front bed?"

His chin quivered. He swallowed.

"Elgin, it's the first day of March today!" She tugged on his arm like a little kid. "It's March. Spring is coming!" She ignored the three feet of snow on the ground and the porch thermometer at minus fifteen degrees.

He lifted his chin to still it, water smudging the blue of his eyes. "Is it?"

"It's March!" she said again for some reason. He stood immobilized, staring at the plants. A hostage being told today's torture session was the last. "It's March! March! March!"

Greta started clapping in time to the words. *March, March, March.* Elgin smiled, one side of his mouth tugging upward. She danced around the kitchen, clapping, chanting. Elgin joined in the clapping, laughing with her. Ash stood by the stove, his mouth hanging open. *March, March, March.* February had passed. They had survived.

"It's going to be okay." She hugged Elgin, cradled his bones. "We're going to be okay."

Ash looked away as they wiped their eyes, sniffled.

After a minute Elgin straightened and said, "This calls for a celebration."

SEVENTEEN

"Greta, come in! Put on some shorts! We're making a frittata."
Elgin brandished a spatula and turned back to the stove, Ash
by his side. Nate sat at the kitchen table, flipping through
the deck of cards.

"I'm good. Thanks."

Greta dropped the shopping bags in front of Nate,
flexing her fingers where the handles had dug in. Then
she surveyed the two butts side by side at the stove, Elgin
wearing lime green today and Ash in some kind of Hawaiian-
print Bermuda shorts.

"Ash, are those—" she began.

"Not a word, Greta," Ash warned over his shoulder.
"Not after this morning."

"Fair enough." She stifled a laugh, but they had already
turned back to the frittata. "I found everything you wanted."
They had sent her to pick up the missing groceries for dinner.
Ash had suggested they make lamb and invite Alice. Greta
tried to give him a *really?* look, but he wouldn't meet her eye.

In the end, Elgin didn't want lamb but invited Alice anyway, and Nate too. Greta hoped Nate wouldn't mention anything about her "nightmare."

An hour later, Greta, Ash and Nate stood gaping as Elgin emerged from his room wearing a baggy pair of black pants and loose button-up shirt. In the silence Elgin said, "Alice has instructed me to wear proper clothes. She's bringing a friend."

"Well"—Greta cleared her throat—"you look nice."

Elgin smoothed the buttons on the front of his shirt before stepping back into the kitchen. As they arranged food on the table—the frittata, mixed-greens salad with balsamic dressing, salmon, and mushroom risotto—Alice and her friend walked through the door.

Ash started making some crack about her just showing up for the food, but his words dropped off midsentence. Greta, her back to the door, set down the napkins and followed his eyes. Alice hadn't just brought a friend. She'd brought a *boy*friend, or a friend who was a boy, with a black leather jacket and cheekbones. She'd brought Johnny Depp from thirty years ago.

"Everyone, this is Kai. He's my roommate's brother." She smiled at him as he rested his hand on the small of her back. So a *boyfriend*.

Elgin stepped forward to shake his hand. Greta was glad he'd put on pants. How many former boyfriends had dumped Alice after that initial introduction? Then Elgin waved everyone over to the table. Alice ended up between Ash and Kai. Greta and Nate sat across from them, and Elgin took the head of the table. A shrunken patriarch.

Most of the conversation revolved around Kai. He liked cats, was thinking of going vegan and had just written a book.

"What's the book about?" Nate asked, shoveling in the risotto.

"It's basically about unrequited love," Kai said, laying down his fork to brush a lock of hair off his cheekbone.

"That sounds like a good universal theme." Elgin chuckled. "Haven't we all loved somebody we can't have?"

Nate glanced at Ash, and Ash at Alice. Alice's eyes flicked to Kai, and he took that moment to check his phone beside his plate. Greta tried to dodge a wave of anger, while Elgin poured himself a glass of wine and missed the whole thing.

Then Kai and Alice—talking over each other—told them about a song they had written together. ("Kai plays the guitar like B.B. King.") It incorporated the science of teeth with analogies of betrayal. Two WTF lines were etched deep between Ash's eyebrows.

Elgin nodded as if this were the most logical thing in the world. "Yes, I see that," he said. "Something could be said, as well, about baby teeth representing the foundations of trust and not being needed as relationships grow." He took a sip of wine and leaned back in his chair, gazing over their heads.

Ash slipped away when Kai, Alice and Elgin poured coffee and hunkered down at the table. Nate and Greta followed him and flopped on the sofa. Greta shifted to one side and motioned for Ash to sit between them. "Welcome to the friend zone," she said. "Plenty of room here."

Nate and Greta sank toward the middle as Ash dropped between them. "That guy's a dick," he said.

"Probably," Greta said, "but at least he's reached the age of majority."

Ash made a sneering face but didn't hold it for long.

"Would you rather," Nate began, "listen to Kai's song on a loop for twenty-four hours straight or go skinny-dipping in Pigeon Lake at the height of algae season? Consider the itch."

"The lake," both Ash and Greta answered. She could stand in solidarity by dissing Kai. Besides, the song sounded like crap.

"Would you rather"—Greta did this one for Ash—"read Kai's book about unrequited love or pepper spray yourself in the eye?

"Pepper spray."

"Would you rather"—Ash looked back and forth between them—"get a free flight to anywhere in the world, sitting next to Kai the whole way, or stay home and clean all the porta potties at the Fringe Festival?"

"Porta potties." Nate nodded.

"Definitely," Greta said.

Poor Kai. Greta glanced over at him, smiling good-naturedly over his coffee. Just waiting to save a baby seal or bring world peace with his awkward-analogy music.

Nate looked pleased that his game of Would You Rather had gained so much momentum. "So, Scrabble rematch?" he said, rising from the couch before they could answer.

There was no point in saying no—he'd bring it anyway. He slipped on his boots by the door and streaked across the street in his T-shirt. The streetlights had just turned on.

At the table, the conversation turned to policies on refugees. This should get interesting, Greta thought. It was hard to imagine Elgin turning anyone away. *Civil war? Come live at my house!* By Alice's arm, Greta's phone started to vibrate.

"Nate probably wants to bring Monopoly too," Greta said, nudging Ash's leg. "You get it."

Alice picked up the phone and gave it an underhand toss, which Ash caught. "Hello?" He already sounded annoyed, ready to say no to whatever Nate suggested. The phone fumbled in his hand before his fingers gripped it again. He shot forward to the edge of the cushion. Turning to look at Greta, he enunciated every word, pulling the phone from his ear until he only spoke into the mouthpiece. "Piss off. There's been a coup." Then he hung up.

The conversation at the table died.

"That was Roger," Ash said, dropping the phone onto Nate's empty cushion and leaning back.

Greta found her voice. "Why'd you hang up?!"

"I didn't want to talk to him."

"Maybe *I* wanted to talk to him!"

"What for? *Hey, Dad, how's life been since you abandoned us?*"

"I don't know!" She grasped for an answer, something to throw back at him. What *would* she say to him? "Give me the phone." She pointed to the cushion and waited for Ash to pass it over.

As she brought up Roger's number and pressed *Call*, Ash rose, muttering, and walked to their bedroom. He slammed the door behind him. Next to Elgin, Kai finally seemed at a loss for nuggets of wisdom. Elgin and Alice stared at Greta while Kai looked at them all one by one.

Nate burst through the front door and was instantly silenced by the funereal atmosphere. "What? What's wrong?" He noticed everyone's eyes on Greta and waited too, the Scrabble box under one arm.

The call went straight to voice mail. She disconnected and redialed, her heartbeat thick and heavy in her chest. The same. She chucked the phone back on the cushion. Alice rose from the table and sat beside her. "You okay?" Kai started in again about war.

Greta nodded at Alice. Her solar plexus was wound into a tight knot. Her limbs felt disconnected from each other—a mismatched collection of flesh, bone, blood.

"Maybe he'll call back," Alice said.

Greta nodded, staring at Elgin's new plants. Nate came and sat on her other side.

"I'll play with you guys," Alice said.

Nate set up the game board, something for his hands to do. Greta stared at the tiles in front of her: *cat, mat, pan, man*. Back to first grade for her, her brain incapable of handling two-syllable words. Alice filled Nate in on what had happened, her voice hushed for once, and then arranged the word *axoneme* on the game board. Greta managed *at* before she wandered to the bedroom, snatching the phone on her way.

She found Ash lying on his back on his bed and staring up at the ceiling. For one second they were in the storage closet again, a bare bulb dangling over their heads. Patty raging outside the door.

"Are you mad at me?" she asked, bracing for a fight. "Don't tell me you're actually mad."

Ash turned to look at her, looming over him. "I'm not mad at *you*. I'm mad at *him*." He turned back to the stark ceiling. "Thinks he can come and go as he pleases. It's like he's playing with us. Your only fault is being too nice."

"You don't even know what he was going to say."

"Would it matter?"

Well. Probably not. "Next time let me talk to him and make that decision myself, okay?"

He rolled away, his back to her. "Okay."

Greta sensed his weight, his dark matter, pulling all light from the room. Sucking her toward a black hole. A few hours ago she had seen him in ugly shorts with Elgin, a sign of camaraderie that only made sense at Elgin's house. They were cooking together again. And Nate with them. Ash actually feeling something for Alice. And even though he was pissed about Kai, they'd made a joke out of it. He was okay. She had wrestled so much with her own okayness that she hadn't realized Ash was getting better, in tiny baby steps. Now this. Anger flared against Roger. Was he playing with them, like Ash said?

They went to bed right then, without saying goodnight to anyone. In their clothes. Greta turned off the light but left the phone by her head. Hating Roger but wanting something from him at the same time. After staring at the dark ceiling for what felt like hours, she picked up the phone and texted Roger: **We live upstairs with Elgin now. Call me sometime.** No response. She drifted off in the middle of the night, woken by pinging notifications and game messages. Every time scrambling to check for texts. **You've won twenty gems in Pirate's Cove! Use them now!**

Dawn marked the end of a sleepless marathon. She turned off the sound on the phone and pushed it far away from her. Then she shut the bedroom door behind her and stepped into the kitchen. Fairies had done the dishes in the night. With a mug of tea cradled in her palms, Greta stood at the picture window, squinting at the glare off the snow in the front yard. She didn't have to wait for the sunrise today. Their part of the earth was tilting closer to the sun every day, like Elgin had said. Slowly.

Ash wandered out a few minutes later, walking as if his legs were hollow. Walking like Elgin. Greta stood to meet him, stopping him by the dining-room table.

"Ash." She grabbed his wrists and shook the pulse back into them. "Ashwin."

He looked at her, letting her hold his wrists.

"We are not stopping here, not navel-gazing and wondering what Dad's up to. We will not be destroyed by him or anyone else. We're getting on with our lives. You hear me?"

He swallowed and nodded, standing a little taller.

"I have an idea about school, but I have to talk to someone first."

He nodded again, without asking any questions. Then she led him to Elgin's chair and made him a cup of tea, even though he hated tea. They made a to-do list, Ash volunteering to do the laundry.

Elgin slept for most of the day, emerging only once to use the bathroom and prod his plants. No spatula-brandishing today. No lime-green-Hawaiian-print euphoria at the stove. Greta watched him fade in and out of the room, feeling a little embarrassed for herself. On one level, she knew it wasn't that simple. *Here are some daffodils and a nice meal. Ta-da! Depression cured!* On the other hand, she'd kind of hoped. He'd had a good day. That was something.

In the late afternoon Greta parked herself on Nate's porch steps, watching for Rebus. At minus five degrees, she barely needed her coat. Even the snow looked dull—white socks after summer camp—probably knowing it would melt soon. Then storm, then melt, then storm, then melt for another two months. Swing between minus twenty and plus twenty.

Rebus pulled into the driveway a few minutes later. Nate climbed out of the driver's side—practically a carnival act, with his long legs—and didn't seem surprised to find Greta waiting there.

"I have a plan for school, Nate," she told him.

"Excellent!" He crushed her in a giant hug.

She smiled into his shoulder.

. . . .

After supper Greta turned down Nate and Ash's invitation to go to West Edmonton Mall with them, her night of phone stalking having caught up with her. She dozed on the couch, her body deadweight while her mind meandered. It tested, stepping gingerly on a stack of images her brain threw at her. Roger. A million live nerves connected to that one. A pang, something sore and tender, attached to him. But also strength—hers and Ash's. A tiny triumph. Patty. Her brain wouldn't even engage—a jag of anger. Then a savage cutting loose. Not their problem anymore. Elgin, Alice, Nate. Something warm there. Their school, West Edmonton High. Greta felt the pang, that tender bruise, and waited for resiliency to offer up some small triumph. Instead, the sensation fell like a rock down a well. Falling. Falling. Never landing. Her body woke a little. Something unfinished there. A taste in her mouth like after a nosebleed. Had Priya been right about her giving up too easily?

She let herself think of them—Dylan, Rachel, Matt, even Sam and Angus—picture their faces, remember their words, their expressions. The way they laughed, both with her and at her. Her gut twisted tight again, all those shards stirring and pinching. But also. But also. Sepia along the border of everything, ebbing over the other colors, subtle. Shame. Greta recognized it, though her anger drove it into hiding. *Still?* What more could she do? She rejected it, called it out, raged at it. But it always crept back. Not so bold now—more of an odor, a trace.

Greta stood, wanting to move but bound by the size of Elgin's living room, his jungle of plants. She ended up shifting in a circle, trapped by those walls of stone and ivy again. Would time dry up the shame? Another talk with Priya? The hurt would remain, she knew. For how long, she didn't know. But the shame? She couldn't accept it, held captive by it even as she rejected it.

Greta mentally paced as she lay in bed, even after Ash crept in without turning on the light. Had she made a mistake leaving West Edmonton High? The thought of going back was like stepping in front of a charging semi, all headlights and rumble. How would that help anything? She checked the time on her phone. One AM. Anxiety stirred as Greta inhaled and exhaled. She knew what to do. And even as she dreaded it, her feet finally touched something firm beneath her. The rock cast down the well hit bottom, with a small but definite splash. She would need backup, someone to walk beside her, prop up her shoulder. Ash? Not unless she wanted to leave a trail of broken limbs. Her mind scanned through names and faces—a short list. Someone strong.

There. Yes. She sent a text.

EIGHTEEN

Greta went to school an hour before classes ended for the day in order to to see the guidance counselor, Mr. Abbott. She needed to know if her plan to finish the school year was feasible. She said something vague about there being a lot going on at home. When he probed for more details, she added, "It's personal," and stared at the floor until he got on with withdrawing her from her courses. That was the easy part—something solid checked off her list. Part one finished, she waited by the front door of the school for part two. Terror beat her sense of satisfaction to death in less than a minute. She had to leave. Vomit roiled at the base of her throat—she could taste it.

Sauntering from the bus stop, Alice wore a bag over one shoulder and a black leather mini. Sandy at the end of *Grease*, all badass, sidestepping puddles leaking from the slushy March snowbanks on either side of the walkway. She sized up the school, from the silver letters mounted on a brick wall to the arched doorway, a look of distaste on her face.

"What are we doing here?" she asked, oblivious to the fact that Greta was about to wet her pants. "Are you trying to give me flashbacks?"

"You went to this school?"

"For a year. Then whats-his-face expelled me. Mr. Fletcher. Is he still around?"

Greta shook her head no.

"That's good. That guy *liked* kids a little too much, if you know what I mean." She looked at Greta's face. "You okay?"

Greta shook her head again. "I need to do something, for..." For what again? "...closure." It came out as a croak. "But I'm not sure now. What if it makes things worse?"

"Do what you need to, girl," Alice said as she walked toward the door, Greta still immobilized behind her. "And why am I here?"

Greta caught up with her, nearly stepping on her suede boots. "Can you just stand beside me? And don't ask any questions." The last thing she wanted was to explain the whole ugly story to Alice in the middle of the hallway at West Edmonton High.

Alice looked puzzled for a second, shrugged, then swung open the door. "FYI, I'm pretty good with spray paint too."

"It's not that kind of closure. Follow me." In the foyer, the bell rang, signaling the end of the day. "We need to get to the second floor, by the chem lab."

Alice matched her steps to Greta's. As they strode past the office, Alice gave the finger to the Visitors Report to Office sign. "That old bat's still there," she said, peeking in the window on the office door. They pushed through the stream of bodies on the stairs, all going down as they went up. Greta panicked as they slowed. Taking too long. It might all be for nothing. Traffic cleared at the top of the stairwell, and they surged forward again. She moved like an Olympic speed walker until she saw them, then reverted to the dream in which she trudged through wet cement while being chased by wild dogs.

Alice charged ahead before doubling back. "What are you doing?"

"Uh…"

Alice looped her arm through Greta's. "You lead the way. Do what you came to do." The warmth of her skin charged Greta's body, moving it again. Ahead, three backs faced the hallway traffic, converged on an open locker: Rachel, Priya and Sam. Rachel reached for a book, her head turned to Priya. Sam saw Greta and Alice first, snapping her body around to face them. Her mouth fell open, but no sound came out. Then Rachel. Then Priya. Like they had rehearsed it. After a second Sam stayed blank. Rachel rolled her eyes, and Priya smiled like Maleficent. They all eyed Alice standing behind Greta.

"Greta—" Rachel started to say, her tone already tired.

"You were a shitty friend," Greta said. A few people paused, slowing their steps as they passed. Pretended not to stare. Rachel's face like she'd been slapped. "It's not okay that you blame me for getting raped, but I can't change that."

Rachel's eyes flicked to the people walking in slow motion. She opened her mouth to speak, but Greta started again. "You left me in the middle of nowhere because I wouldn't sleep with your friend." She swallowed to steady her voice.

Priya jumped in. "Seriously, Rachel?" She made eye contact with a few people passing by. "Can you imagine if that gets out?" She made a cringe-y face, then winked at Greta when they turned away. Sam looked like she wanted to leave but didn't quite know how, confrontation pinning her there.

Rachel's face reddened, her eyes darting around. "Greta, can we talk about this—"

"Whether you believe me about Dylan or not, what happened afterward is on you. You're the kind of person who would abandon, even endanger, a friend because a boy told you to. You should look at that."

Two twelfth-grade girls stopped to watch until Rachel snapped, "Do you mind?" Then she slammed her locker shut and tried to step around Greta.

Greta maneuvered to block her, anger moving her legs. She wasn't done yet. "Am I making you uncomfortable, Rachel?" Alice shifted to Greta's side, crossing her arms. So cool and controlled, all blond hair and leather. Greta envied everything about Alice in that second.

Greta continued. "And even though I think you're the worst kind of person, I hope it never happens to you—any of what you and your friends put me through. Shame on you, Rachel. Not me. *You.*" She'd hoisted it back on Rachel. She wouldn't carry it for her anymore.

Then Greta backed away, pulling Alice with her. Her heart swelled her whole body to twice its normal size, hardened her core.

"Greta," Rachel called out, her voice somewhere between a yelp and a swallow. Greta looked back over her shoulder.

Rachel's face glowed bright red. She looked small, for the first time ever. All ninety pounds and five feet, two inches of her. "I'm sorry."

Greta nodded. "I'll take that into consideration."

"Greta"—Priya raised a finger for her to wait—"I'm on the grad committee, and we're planning a mock casino for our grad party. All the money we raise is going to charities that support victims of sexual assault. I thought you might like to know." She looked at Rachel and Sam before speaking again. "I considered telling people that Dylan was responsible for every case of herpes in this school, but then I remembered how it felt to have lies spread about me." Her eyes rested on Rachel, whose face turned a deeper red. "I didn't want to sink to that level."

"Thanks for that, Priya," Greta said, smiling, and steered Alice away.

This time Alice fell behind, jogging to catch up. "Okay, I'm starting to understand."

Greta looked straight ahead. She couldn't stop now, not to talk, dissect, explain. She had to move while her core held firm.

"Where are we going now?" Alice asked.

"To the gym."

Alice matched Greta's pace, and they jostled students out of their way—those who didn't move quickly enough.

"I'm liking this new Greta," Alice said as a muscly guy flattened himself against his locker to avoid them. "Are you sure about the spray paint?"

Greta ignored her and kept walking, her legs knowing the way. Her feet a blur down the stairs. Traffic thinned toward the gym. She strode forward until she heard the smack of balls against the floor, the echoing shouts. Greta stopped, Alice plowing into her.

"What? Why have you stopped?" Alice asked.

"I think I'm going to be sick."

"No you're not."

"No, really." Saliva pooled at the back of her mouth, her belly a heavy sponge. She swallowed hard and bent forward, her hands on her knees. Sweat out of nowhere.

"You're going to finish this. I can't wait!" Alice beamed.

Maybe Ash would've been better, Greta thought, broken limbs or not. She drew a few breaths to steady her stomach and pulled herself upright, using Alice's shoulder as a crutch. But she didn't let go. She reached for Alice's hand, squeezing her palm tightly. Hand in hand, they walked through the gym doors.

Practice hadn't started yet. The coach talk-shouted into a cell phone by the bleachers. Half the basketball team milled around the court, haphazardly taking shots at the same time, their balls ricocheting off the rim of the hoop. A guy built like a bull moose did an under-the-leg-and-over-the-shoulder trick with his ball.

Greta knew the moment they saw her by the silence that fell on them, one by one, balls dribbling to a stop or held in hands. She didn't know what they knew or what they'd been told, but they definitely recognized her as Ash's sister. Dylan, near the center of the gym, chucked his ball into the bleachers and walked toward her. A greenish-purple bruise distorted one cheekbone, and his lower lip was split and swollen. She saw him now—a trinket, plastic painted gold. Greta laced her fingers through Alice's, squeezing all the blood from them.

As Dylan approached, he eyed her hand in Alice's and smirked. "Well, that explains a lot." Around him, his teammates hooted. Alice didn't even blink.

Greta's face warmed. She tried to absorb Alice's energy, her courage. Dylan had taken the upper hand. She knew it. There would be no red-faced apology from this one.

"Dylan." Her voice came out quiet, reasonable, like she had loaned him twenty bucks and needed it back. While being circled by twenty great white sharks. He cocked his head, amused. "Dylan, if someone isn't in a state to say yes or no"—her voice quavered—"the answer—"

"Greta," Dylan said, bored, "it wasn't even that good. Don't flatter yourself." His teammates snorted, some looking at the floor and some straight in her face, wanting to see her crumble and fall.

Alice turned and whispered in Greta's ear, "Permission to speak?"

Greta nodded, swallowing against the lump rising in her throat.

"Hey, dipshit!" Alice shook off Greta's hand and stepped forward, shoving Dylan's shoulders. He stumbled back, caught off guard by the angry-princess look-alike. "Did you hear what she said?" She stepped close to his face, every muscle in her neck strained. "We'll make it simple so even you can understand. If a person can't say yes or no, the answer's always no!"

She tried to shove him again, but he caught her wrists, repelling her. "Get your hands off me!" His fists twitched in her direction, like he wanted to deck her but couldn't.

"That's probably what every girl you've slept with was thinking too," Alice said.

The guy who had done the ball tricks started to laugh and then swallowed it. "Oh, burn," he muttered.

Greta guessed he wasn't Dylan's biggest fan.

"Get out of here!" Dylan shouted at them. The coach looked up from his phone call, frowning.

"Can't wait," Alice drawled. "The smell's getting to me. Close the deal, Greta."

Greta cleared her throat and stepped forward, her hands trembling but legs planted firmly on the ground. The earth held her up. She didn't need Alice anymore. She deserved to stand there, deserved to be heard. The faces around them blurred until only Dylan's sneer remained. "Shame on you, Dylan." No more timid schoolgirl. She'd carried it for him too long. "Not on me. On *you.*" Not hers anymore.

She turned as his face changed color, shape—a chemical reaction—but didn't wait to see where it would end. A villain who shifted from human to monster. Alice reached for her hand again, and Greta grasped it. They swung arms as shouting erupted behind them. Greta blocked out the words—they weren't hers, and she refused them. The noise clipped as the heavy gym doors swung closed. No more balls against the floor. More like a bar brawl.

Their legs moved in sync down the hallway. Greta waited for demons in basketball uniforms to swirl around her, spit in her face, but they didn't. Maybe they carried the shame now. Maybe *he* did.

They pushed through the front doors, Greta's legs moving forward until Alice pulled her to a stop. She turned Greta's shoulders to face her, looking at her eye to eye. "That was brave, Greta. You were brave."

Alice pulled Greta close and held her until her bones stopped rattling, until the blood slowed in her veins. Her body throbbed, from her heart to the bottom of her gut. Free from shame but ripped wide open. When Greta could breathe again, Alice held her at arm's length and said, "Now you move forward."

Greta nodded. *Forward.*

They joined hands and walked to the bus stop, West Edmonton High a dumpster fire burning behind them.

NINETEEN

On the bus, adrenaline leaked from Greta's body, leaving it a deflated bike tire. She slumped against Alice's shoulder, neither of them speaking. A tentative peace settled over her. Greta knew it would vanish the minute they stepped off the bus and attempted this "forward," but for now she let it cradle her. Alice squeezed her hand and let go, lost in her own thoughts.

From the bus stop they walked home in silence, the slushy edges of piled snow starting to harden as the temperature dropped in the late afternoon. Before they reached Elgin's house, Greta said, "Thank you, Alice. It made a huge difference, having you there."

"Pfft. You would've done fine on your own, believe me. But you're welcome." She looked sideways at Greta and smiled. "You impressed me, you know? Maybe I should've done more of that myself." The smiled dropped from her face. Greta figured she was probably remembering her own lineup of people to tell off. "If you ever want to talk, Greta, about…"

Her head swayed, searching for the right word. "You know, just let me know."

"Thanks." Greta looked straight ahead and stepped onto Elgin's front path. She didn't know when she'd want to talk about it again, but if she did, Alice would be top of the list. And she probably owed Priya a bouquet of flowers.

Before they reached the door, Alice held her back again. "A friend of mine used to see someone at the Sexual Assault Center." She pulled out her phone and googled it. "They have a twenty-four-hour crisis line and counseling. I'll text you the info."

Greta looked at the website and nodded. She didn't know yet if she was interested. But after today, people— Ash, Priya, Alice, maybe someone from this center—stood in her corner. People to say, I believe you. "Thank you, Alice. I'll remember that."

. · · .

In the house, Nate leaned over Ash's shoulder, both of them gazing at the screen of Nate's laptop on Elgin's kitchen table. Ash gave Greta a cranky-grandpa look as she slid off her boots.

"A note, Greta. That's all I ask." He managed a smile at Alice before turning back to the screen. "Now look." He pointed for Nate. "It won't remember my username."

"Ash." Greta stood beside him. "Enjoy the computer games now, because you and I are going to summer school."

"Say what?"

"I saw Mr. Abbott today, and he registered us in math and social studies at Masters Continuing Education in July and August. They don't offer languages then, so we'll have to do French online."

"But I don't even need French!"

"I couldn't convince him otherwise, not after your inspiring 'I need to be a French teacher' speech."

Ash sighed and leaned back in his chair. "Fine."

"You're welcome."

He smiled. "Thank you, Greta." They would finish two months late, without the stupid ceremony, but they would graduate.

Then the last of her energy evaporated. She slipped away, needing a quiet space. While her muscles felt spent, weak, her frame held tall, strong. She'd lifted a car over her head and flung the whole thing into a gully. Collapsing on Ash's bed, Greta closed her eyes. Rachel's and Dylan's red faces, their sputtering, their anger and shame—no longer her own. She should start wearing a cape.

Alice ended up staying for supper, Elgin pleased to find her there when he came out of his room. He rushed (Elgin-style, so more like a fast shuffle) through his plant care to be ready to sit and eat with them. Nate made taco soup, half of the ingredients pilfered from his own kitchen. "I'll keep a bowl for my dad," he said, glancing guiltily in the direction of his house.

By nine o'clock Greta's eyelids only opened halfway. "I'm going to bed," she told the others, who were playing cards at the kitchen table. Nate looked up and smiled—"Good night, Greta!"—while the rest of them mumbled into their cards.

She fell asleep the second she closed her eyes, not even stopping to top up her air mattress. The floor against her hip was not a deterrent at all. A dead, dreamless sleep, not touched by the occasional shout from the kitchen. Then awake. She blinked into the dark. Had she just closed her eyes? She reached up to the bed and felt Ash's leg. He'd come in without waking her. In the kitchen, silence, and darkness from the crack under the door. Was it morning? The heaviness in her body said no. She'd been woken by something—a noise. The light flashed on the phone beside her pillow. Annoyed that she'd forgotten to turn off the sound, she reached for it and saw the text notification. Wide awake. Who was texting her at—she checked the time—12:30 AM? She clicked on the message icon.

I'm downstairs.

A jolt of fear. From? *Dad.* A second jolt—something she couldn't even name. Another message opened as she held the phone. **Can you come down and talk to me?** She stared at the words. Some kind of trap? But this was her dad…possibly with Patty. She could handle seeing Roger. Greta knew with 100 percent certainty that she never again wanted to lay eyes on Patty. Never breathe the same air. Never stand within the same four walls. No compromise, no promise of change, would move her. Never again. Something had shifted after today. Roger? Still murky. Greta reached to shake Ash's leg but jerked her hand back before it touched him.

If she woke him, she'd never know why Roger was texting her from their basement. She wanted to know, she realized, and see his face again.

Be right there, she texted back, then switched the phone to silent in case he responded. She couldn't risk this being the one time that Ash, who slept like he'd been euthanized, woke up and followed her. She padded out the door and through the kitchen, still wearing her clothes from earlier that day. When her hand touched the door handle to the basement staircase, her chest exploded, catching her breath in her throat. Her dad was at the bottom of those stairs. Her bare feet registered the shift in temperature with each dropping step, dread now mixed with the cocktail of fear, excitement and adrenaline pumping through her blood.

Roger. He sat on the sofa with a blanket across his lap, wearing a baseball cap and a winter jacket. Only Roger. Silver in his unshaven whiskers, joy on his face. She loved it. Hated it. Pausing at the bottom of the stairs, she checked him over. He stood up, the blanket dropping to the floor, wearing a pair of jeans that looked like they could walk to the laundry on their own. He was shorter than she remembered, thinner. Older. One of those rubbery sponge toys that grows in water but shrivels outside it. Could a person shrink in two months?

"Greta!" Roger burst toward her, his feet getting tangled in the blanket. Then he stopped, either because of the blanket or because she didn't budge.

"Dad." She nodded in response. Cool. Formal. She would give him nothing.

"You're looking well." He grinned, his Adam's apple working against the emotion in his throat.

No thanks to you. She stepped forward into the living room, the furniture around them just a dusty set from a play they'd seen long ago. She held every emotion in tight, all her defences up. And still fought the impulse to touch him. Like a piece of her own flesh returned to her body again. Greta wanted to feel his breath, his warmth. That groove between his eyebrows so much like Ash's. Roger, back from the dead.

"How are you?" Roger stammered. "How's—"

"You left us. You chose her." A robot speaking.

Roger swallowed, his tears so immediate that Greta wondered if somehow the body heard the words before they reached his ears. "Yes," he croaked. "I did."

She observed him, his mouth twisting and hands trembling. Greta knew the next question should be *why*, but she didn't want to provide the platform for his remorse. He'd have to do the work all by himself. She'd provide no stepping stone for his sad story.

"It was a mistake. I'm so sorry." He barely got the words out.

Greta stepped closer and laid her fingers on his hand, just to see if she could still the trembling. Curious. No. Roger took it as a sign of affection and grasped her hand tightly. She recoiled. He flinched.

"What do you want, Dad?" she asked.

"I just wanted...I wanted..." As though her question caught him off guard. "Well, Patty and I are done. That's over."

That woke Greta up a bit. "So you thought you could come back to me and Ash now that your first choice fell through?"

"No!" His eyes burned fiercely. "It's not like that. Patty and I were only together for a month after I saw you in Whitecourt. I told her it was over." He looked away and struggled for composure before speaking again. "Hated myself."

A spark lit in Greta. "Wait, you left her a month ago and just show up *now*?"

Roger nodded. "I didn't feel I could come back again until I had something to offer you. Not after leaving like that."

"You could've called!"

"And said what?"

"I don't know!" *Ding dong the witch is dead?* " 'I'm alive'? 'I still love you'?"

"I wanted to have something to show you I'm committed to us as a family."

Greta shook her head. "And what is this big plan?" At this point, he could've produced a diamond-studded tiara and she would've spat on it.

"Well," Roger began, "you know how we've been saving for a house?"

Greta stared at him without responding.

"I still don't have quite enough for the down payment, but I've found a good place for us. The owner agreed to let us rent for six months until I've saved enough, and then we can buy it. We'll have our own home again, just the three of us."

His face opened—bright, hopeful. She let it sit like that for a minute before answering. "You know what kind of home

I'd like, Dad? One where a father stands up for his kids, instead of offering them as a sacrifice to some lunatic. One where a father doesn't take off"—her inhuman calm shattered— "IN THE MIDDLE OF THE NIGHT, leaving his kids to fend for themselves!" She felt her face distort, a fleck of spittle fly. A deranged person. Roger cowered, crushed. She stepped away to keep from slapping his face.

She backed out of the living room and turned at the bottom of the stairs. Now she had to say it, couldn't help herself. "Why, Dad? Why? You put us in harm's way for seven years and then left us. I'll never understand."

Roger shook his head and rubbed a hand over his mouth. "I guess…I guess I didn't think I could handle losing another wife."

"Do you realize the price you paid? The price Ash and I paid?"

He nodded, his eyes manic. "I'm so sorry, Greta. I'll do whatever you ask to prove I won't let you down again."

Greta continued, ignoring his apology. "First you lost wife number one. Then, in trying to keep wife number two happy, you lost your two children. Then you left your horror of a second wife anyway. Congratulations, Dad. You managed to lose everyone." She turned and ran up the stairs before he could respond.

Thankfully, Elgin wasn't in his chair that night. Greta curled up in hers, shaded by fern leaves, and cried.

TWENTY

She woke to Ash standing over her with a look of concern. "Does everyone take turns falling asleep in these chairs? Got tired of the air mattress?"

Greta smiled at him and tugged his arm toward Elgin's empty chair. "Sit down. I have something to tell you." Then she explained about Roger's text and their brief conversation— his leaving Patty, his house plan and her losing her mind.

Ash sat on the edge of the cushion the whole time, gripping the plushy arms like someone might press *Eject* at any moment. "Unbelievable!" he spat as she finished. Then he jumped from the chair and tried to pace without running into plants. For the level of anxiety in this house, Greta thought, Elgin really needed a bigger living room.

He turned on Greta. "Why didn't you wake me up?"

"So you could do this"—she waved her hand in his direction—"while we tried to have a conversation?"

"It doesn't sound like you were exactly a paragon of patience yourself."

"Shut up," Greta said, but it was halfhearted. Guilt. She had seen Roger wilt under her words. But he deserved it, didn't he? Yes. He'd hurt them and was wrong. So wrong. Then why did she feel a pang thinking about her brutality? She knew the answer even as she asked herself the question. She loved him. On some primal level, it hurt seeing him hurt. All of his wrongs aside, it crushed her to see him old, tired, small, devastated. "He didn't look good, Ash."

"Boo-hoo," Ash said. "How did we look the day we woke up to an empty house?"

She didn't know what to say, how to explain the full-on war waging inside of her.

"Wait." Ash stopped short. "Is he still downstairs?" He didn't wait for her answer before bounding across the kitchen and thumping down the stairs to the basement. Greta trained her ears on the open basement door but didn't get up and follow. Ash's turn. He walked back upstairs with less energy. "No one home."

What did this mean now? Roger still had a key to the basement suite. He could come and go anytime. Was he moving back in? Did Elgin know? And would Elgin still offer to let them stay if Roger came back? Greta suddenly felt unsettled in her seat, like the floor might give way at any moment and drop her back downstairs.

All morning Greta eyed her phone constantly. That was the worst thing about Roger—the coming and going. Here now. Gone again. Maybe her reaction had driven him back to his truck and all the way up to Whitecourt. Her heart dropped at the thought at the same time her head said, *Good*. Ash fidgeted, baking a cake and then scraping it into the garbage because he'd forgotten to add sugar. Elgin slept on.

Greta finally gave up and wandered over to the picture window. She looked out at the yard, smug, like she'd single-handedly orchestrated the beginning of spring. Just above freezing, snow wilting in soft mounds, the sun through the window warm on her arms. It wouldn't last—they all knew it. But until the next snow dump, she could pretend, and maybe see snatches of dead, waterlogged grass—the most beautiful sight in the world.

She and Ash went to Nate's porch around the time school would be finishing and waited until he pulled up in Rebus. Nate stepped out of the car, a line in his forehead. "What's wrong?"

"We're bored," Ash said. "Wanna play Scrabble?"

Nate smiled, like his brainwashing might be paying off after all. On the way inside Greta told him about Roger's midnight visit. A couple of hours later Ash and Greta walked back to Elgin's, thinking of supper and wondering how to broach the subject of Roger with Elgin.

In the entryway, Ash stopped abruptly. Greta plowed into his back. Roger. At the kitchen table with Elgin. Both wearing pants. Elgin smiled like they were guests stepping through his door for the first time. Roger smiled, too, although Greta saw the unease in his eyes. He had to know he was about to tiptoe through a minefield. He'd shaved and changed his shirt, but dark pouches marked his eyes.

Ash bristled. Greta was sure even his arm hair prickled, his arms in gunslinger position. Greta peered around his shoulder. She'd sent Roger away in fury, and he'd come back to fight for them. Relief, a streak of tenderness, then *boom*. Up went the wall, the one that reminded her of everything that smiling face had done. Or hadn't.

Ash spoke first. "What's *he* doing here?" His lips barely moved, drawn tight. He directed the question at Elgin, bypassing Roger.

"Your father and I have been talking for the past hour. Come in, please. This is a family matter."

"I have no father," Ash said, not moving.

Both men blinked at that, Roger sucking in a breath.

"I've asked Alice to come pick me up," Elgin said (which explained the pants), "so you three can have your own heuristic. Remember, it's about finding a functional solution in a less-than-ideal situation."

Greta wasn't sure why he didn't just banish them all back to the basement pit. At that moment, Alice squeezed through the doorway behind them, jamming three people into two square feet. "Um, excuse me," she said, her voice muffled by Greta's shoulder.

"Elgin and Alice stay," Ash said. "Or I go."

Greta wasn't sure if Elgin and Alice wanted to be part of their family's heuristic, especially given the way the first one had gone. Elgin looked to Roger for his thoughts, while Alice brightened the same way she had at the prospect of spray paint. "I'll stay. Who's this?" She wormed her way past Greta and Ash to size up Roger.

"Our father," Greta said, to spare Ash from having to say the word.

"Oh." Her face fell. "You guys are really draining the swamp lately, aren't you?"

"Alice!" This from Elgin.

"What? You know what this guy—"

"Come sit down, all of you." Elgin motioned them to the table and pulled out chairs for them.

Once they all were sitting, everyone went silent. In family councils with Patty, Ash would pull out things like "I bet you're all wondering why I've called this meeting," until Patty lost it. Now he didn't look in Roger's direction at all.

"So. Your father's back and would like to assume responsibility for you," Elgin began.

"He still owes you money! A month's rent," Ash sputtered. "Not to mention groceries, utilities…" Alice nodded like they were just getting started.

Elgin interjected before Ash could continue. "We've worked out a plan to pay that back. This is about your family now."

"I've signed a lease on a house," Roger said cautiously. Greta had started to wonder if he'd speak at all. "It's available at the end of the month. I'll be ready to put in an offer to buy it by September."

"Give us one good reason we should trust you," Ash said.

Greta leaned forward to hear the answer too. She wanted to believe him—the house, the white picket fence, the happy family—but it felt like another trail of crumbs. Hope, then trauma, then nothing.

"I promise you—"

"Not good enough!" Ash's voice grew stronger, like his words alone could knock Roger flat.

Elgin cleared his throat and stepped in. "Ash. Greta. If I may." Ash clamped his mouth shut. "Maybe I seem like a kind person to you. I try to be. I took you in when you needed it, and I enjoy having you here. Truth be told"—he drew a breath, wilting a little—"I'll miss you when you're gone, but you're not mine to keep."

They waited for him to continue, all digesting his admission.

He continued: "But my Alice here can tell you how many times I've failed as a father, as a human being." Alice focused on the table, her face instantly red. "I can remember at least five times that I completely forgot to pick her up from school, and they had to call me to come get her."

She nodded. "There were seven in the space of two months. Every single time, I stood on the side of the road for an hour, waiting for you."

"Seven. Right. And I forgot her birthday the year Eleanor died. The day came and went, and she sat in her room waiting for party guests to arrive." He swallowed hard at that memory.

"Every year, Dad," Alice said, her voice thick. "You've forgotten my birthday every year since Mom died."

"Yes. Every year." He shrank smaller in his skin, both he and Roger almost husks now.

"And that one time you picked me up from school in your boxers, and I got teased so bad that I tried to get expelled so I wouldn't have to go back. After that I begged you to let me take the bus."

"You never told me that." He swiveled to look at her.

She nodded, blinking back tears. "Or the time I woke up in the night and found you'd wandered out in the snow, and I had to ask the neighbors to help get you back inside. Ringing doorbells at two in the morning."

Elgin's eyebrows knit together, and Greta knew they had stumbled onto failings he didn't even remember.

"But at least he never left you," Ash said, like this tipped the scale the other way.

"He left me in every other way except the physical. I could reach out and touch him—yes—but that doesn't mean he was with me."

Elgin looked like he'd been struck. "I'm sorry, Alice. I will always be sorry for that. I hope I can make it up to you." He struggled to collect himself, not sure where to look now. "My point is, Ash and Greta, that even people who love you make mistakes—terrible mistakes—and disappoint and embarrass you. But if you can see some good in me, a flawed person, can you also see it in your father?"

Silence. Eyes traveled from face to face. Ash deflated to his normal size, his face drooping, followed by his shoulders. Greta looked back and forth between Roger and Ash. *Yes.* Part of her wanted to believe—the part that remembered every piggyback ride, every time she had wiggled in excitement while riding in the cab of his truck. Roger, so much a part of her that she heard his voice whenever she put on her warm jacket or saw a semi drive by.

"Dad." Beside her, Ash spoke, his voice finally calm. "Dad, it killed us when you left. In a million years, I never thought you'd do that."

Roger nodded, waiting. Greta recognized the look on his face. Shame.

"And I just don't think I can trust you again."

With that, Greta saw three balls lined up for the same hoop ricochet off each other and scatter.

TWENTY-ONE

The heuristic fell apart after Ash got up and left. Everyone stood, knowing a door had closed. Roger stepped out from his chair and leaned over to hug Greta. For one second she let herself lean into him and remember. One second. Then she followed Ash, leaving Elgin and Alice to the aftermath.

On the table the next morning, they found a note written in Sharpie on the back of a flyer: *I will wait for you there, always,* along with the new house address. Greta reached for it, but Ash crumpled it in his hands, his edges and prickles back again.

"Give it to me," she said, taking it and smoothing it flat. "Maybe I want to see it."

"What for?" Ash asked. "Elgin won't be there to step in when Dad bails again."

"What makes you think he'll bail again?"

Ash shrugged. "I never thought he'd do it the first time. Maybe he'll fall in love with Patty's twin sister. Too much pressure on the job. A sudden gambling addiction. It could be anything."

"I don't know, Ash. What if he's sincere?"

"Greta." Ash stepped close, into her space. "Are you thinking of going with him? Would you go without me?"

She saw the hurt, the alarm, in his eyes.

"No, Ash." She stepped back. "I don't know."

He watched her without moving, his eyebrows pinched together. After a full minute of silence, he said, "I won't ask you not to live with Dad, but I don't trust him. And I'll...I'll miss you."

Greta kept her head turned to spare him the embarrassment of eye contact, knowing how much that last sentence had cost him to say. "Don't worry about it, Ash. Okay?" She stuck the flyer on the fridge with a Dan's Plumbing magnet. "Where do you think we should go then? We can't stay with Elgin forever, especially now that Dad's back."

"I don't know." Ash shrugged. "I'm sure Elgin will let us stay a little longer, or Nate might let us crash there until Aunt Lori gets back. We wouldn't end up under a bridge."

"But think about it, Ash. We could be together again, the three of us. We haven't had that chance in seven years." She couldn't stop picturing the house, sitting around a dinner table with Ash and Roger. A conversation without Patty's dog-whistle-pitched voice. For one second, the anger in Ash's face fell away, and she knew he saw it too. "Just...what if..." She let it hang.

Ash shook his head, the moment gone. "I'll be around no matter what you decide, Greta, but I'm not ready to go with him. Not yet."

. · · · .

The last weekend in March, they all pitched in to help move Roger's stuff out of the basement. Greta shrank from it, the residue of Patty all over everything. She considered tacking a Free Stuff sign on it and dumping it at the end of the driveway. Ash offered to help load the moving van as long as Roger wasn't there, so Roger waited inside the van with the radio on. Elgin stood on the front path to supervise, saying things like "lift from the knees" as Ash and Nate hoisted mattresses into the back of the van. Greta and Alice packed the contents of closets and drawers into boxes, starting with the bedrooms. Chased away spiders.

They moved on to the kitchen as Ash and Nate came in for a drink of water, breathless and sweaty. Tracking mud across the hardwood. Alice leaned against the oven door, then did a double take. "Aw, look at this itty-bitty…" She swung the door open and bent down, peering inside. "How the heck did you guys fit anything inside this?"

"Oh, it served its purpose." Ash smiled at Greta. He passed by Alice to get a refill from the sink and nudged her hip, tipping her toward the open oven. "Careful now. Don't fall in."

Alice swatted his leg and straightened. "Very funny."

Greta tapped on Roger's window when they'd finished. "All done." His work buddies were coming to help unload at the new house.

Roger smiled. "Want to come along, Greta? I'll show you the house. You can get first dibs on your room...in case... you know."

Greta paused, looking at Roger and then back at Ash, Elgin, Nate and Alice. They had already agreed to meet at Elgin's house for dinner the first Sunday of every month, regardless of where everyone lived. The next day she and Ash would move in with Aunt Lori, and Elgin would look for renters for the basement suite. She stood on the threshold of something new, but she couldn't picture the coming months. With Ash at Aunt Lori's? A new home, a new life, with her dad? Could she choose that path if it meant leaving Ash behind? Would he eventually follow if she stepped away first?

"I'll just look at it," Greta told Roger. "You'll drive me back after they unload?"

Roger nodded, turning the key in the ignition.

She walked back toward the house as Roger rolled up the window behind her. "I just want to see it, Ash. Nothing decided."

Ash stepped forward —a conversation just for the two of them. "You can forgive him, just like that?" An accusation there, also edged in wonder.

"No, Ash. I don't forgive him. Not yet." With Roger, the wall came and went, sometimes falling at surprising times, allowing her to joke in a text or return his calls. Other times it sprang up fast, and she couldn't even look at him or hear his voice. "But I guess the difference between us is"—she paused—"I *want* to forgive him."

Ash watched her face, a heavy silence between them. Then he nodded, wiping his hands on his dusty T-shirt. "Okay. See you in a bit." He looked away. She knew he'd never say "pick me" or plead or pressure, but she saw his hurt expression when he didn't snap it to neutral fast enough. It was supposed to be her and him looking out for each other, the only sure thing out of 7.5 billion people. She hadn't forgotten.

Riding in the van with Roger, Greta watched him sing along to country songs. Wall up. She didn't sing with him— a guilty pleasure she wouldn't admit to under torture. He tapped his thumbs against the steering wheel and missed every high note. Seeing him happy, Greta wondered what he'd said to Patty the last time they spoke. Maybe someday she'd be ready for— even find satisfaction in—that conversation. At this point, any thoughts of Patty just reinforced those hefty bricks between her and Roger.

Roger took Anthony Henday Drive to north Edmonton and weaved through a residential area. They drove down narrow streets, a mixture of older homes and new infill. He pulled up in front of a bungalow with light yellow siding, white trim and a flower bed full of dead, soggy plants by the front porch. The front lawn was a neat rectangle.

"Home sweet home," Roger said, swinging his legs out of the driver's seat.

Greta followed him onto the front porch and waited while he dug out the key. The house reminded her of Elgin's, only newer and without ferns. In the living room, a large picture window overlooked the front lawn. She mentally positioned her and Elgin's chairs, then felt a thin stab. Was it so impossible that Elgin—and Ash, Nate and Alice—might come to Roger's house sometime? A new path, a new gathering place?

A wall separated the dining room and kitchen, although a small table would fit in the kitchen too. "No dishwasher yet," Roger said, pointing to the gap in the cupboards. Greta noted the standard-sized oven, electric. Roger, as if reading her mind, added, "The furnace is new."

Greta trailed behind Roger through three bedrooms, all with laminate flooring and small rectangular windows. "You or Ash can have this one," he said, pointing to the largest of the three. "It's just me now."

"Let's give it to Ash," Greta answered, a little too easily. "If he…if we come," she added, stepping out of the room.

Roger closed the door behind them, as if preserving it. "Yes, Ash's room." He checked a text on his phone. "My buddies will be here in five."

They wandered back to the living room. Greta pressed her hands against the window, leaving the shape of her print. She resisted the urge to press her nose against the glass, too, some forgotten habit. She inspected the mud-brown grass, the remnants of the last snow still lumped randomly across the lawn.

"Dad"—Greta heard him move behind her—"didn't we live in a house like this when I was little?"

Roger gave a laugh of surprise. "You remember? I think that's why I liked this one, actually. They're very similar. You were probably three or four."

"I remember moving in," she said. "An empty room like this. We sat on the floor to eat. Mom was…mad about something." She pictured Diana's face, usually calm but pinched in irritation as she talked to Roger.

"I gave you donuts," Roger said. "We went through a Tim Hortons drive-through on the way over, so you didn't want your sandwiches and vegetables." He chuckled at the memory. "She had packed a lunch for nothing."

Greta smiled at the thought of Diana coaxing them to take a few bites of real food. "Yes, she did try to explain things like vitamins and fiber to us, didn't she?" Then she saw her mother tucking her and Ash into sleeping bags at night, blankets spread beneath them, sorting through boxes with Roger by the light of a floor lamp.

"I remember," Greta said. Before Mother. Before Family. Some mundane memory of her mom getting annoyed with Roger. She remembered it. Roger either didn't hear her or understood that she wouldn't want to explain. He stood next to her at the window, smiling at the memory in his own head.

Greta could see it all again. Her, Ash and Roger sitting on the floor, trying to eat Chinese food with chopsticks, not knowing which box held the forks. She could see them slouched on the sofa watching *Quiz Kings*, snowflakes falling outside the window. She saw them. They argued about whose turn it was to clean the bathroom. They made scrambled eggs for each other. They sat on the back porch on summer days, sticky hot, and couldn't imagine a season when snow would fall again.

But that vision included Ash. Her joy dropped away. If she asked him, he'd walk away from anyone—Roger, Nate, Alice, Elgin, Aunt Lori—to sleep in a ditch by her side. She traded places with him in her mind, tried to imagine Ash shopping around for another home while she couch surfed at Aunt Lori's. He'd never. She felt a twinge of guilt. She didn't totally understand his anger, but she understood his loyalty to her. They had just dragged each other through a valley of broken glass and vinegar. That counted for something. She'd tell Roger "not yet" when he dropped her off later and do her best to explain. It stung, seeing something that beautiful, that comfortable, and knowing she had to let it go. But there was relief in finally making a decision.

The doorbell rang, and Roger hollered, "Come in!" He clapped his friends on the shoulders as they came through the door. Greta smiled and squeezed past them, sitting on the edge of the bottom porch step while they hauled in the big furniture.

The end of the sofa dipped close to her head. She ducked to avoid it and the men's clumsy feet as they groped for the next step. She slipped off to the side, by the wilted flower bed, and waited for them to pass. As she settled back on the step, a yellow blur moved in the corner of her eye. Rebus at the curb. Then a shadow up the path, a loping gait, hair flopping over one eye.

Greta smiled. Like she had waved a magic wand and willed him there.

"I'm not making any promises," Ash said before Greta could speak. "And I call dibs on the biggest bedroom." His lips tugged upward in an almost-smile.

"You can have it," she said. That and Chinese food, and *Quiz Kings*, and scrambled eggs and hot summer nights. And every good thing. "I already marked my territory in the other one."

Ash smiled back for a second. Then his face fell serious, as if he was already in the house and starting that conversation with Roger—the one that needed to happen. He gave Greta a nod, squared his shoulders and stepped through the door.

AFTERWORD

Greta's story is just one of many; it does not represent how all survivors experience sexual violence. Trauma affects people differently. In *Trail of Crumbs*, Greta confronts her perpetrator to help her heal and move forward. This may not be the best course of action for every person who has experienced sexual violence. In some cases, confronting the person who has done harm may be retraumatizing or unsafe. There are many ways to go through the healing process, and the person who has experienced sexual violence should get to decide what their process looks like.

If you have been affected by sexual violence and would like to seek help, many resources are available to you. Unsure where to start? In Canada, Kids Help Phone (kidshelpphone.ca or 1-800-668-6868) is a free, anonymous and bilingual professional counseling, information and referral service for young people. The service is available 24/7 by phone, Live Chat and the Always There chat app. In the United States, RAINN (Rape, Abuse & Incest National Network) is a national anti–sexual violence organization (rainn.org or 800-656-4673). There are many other national and local hotlines, organizations and counselors ready to help you.

ACKNOWLEDGMENTS

Thank you, Debbie Watson (counselor extraordinaire), for sharing ideas and insights and for your feedback and encouragement while I wrote this book. The staff at the Sexual Assault Centre of Edmonton was also extremely helpful and supportive. In particular, thanks to Jess Marie for her feedback on a variety of topics!

Thank you to the whole team at Orca: Sarah Harvey (editor extraordinaire), who saw the potential in this story, Teresa Bubela for her cover design, Sofía Bonati for the cover illustration and all the people who work behind the scenes with such professionalism. You truly are a well-oiled machine (with a very human touch!).

Thanks also to Hilary McMahon and Liz Culotti (agents extraordinaire) at Westwood Creative Artists for all their efforts on my behalf.

Thanks to Lisa Wickstrom (friend extraordinaire) for reading an earlier draft of this book, and to Lisa and Karen Wickstrom for any stolen dialogue. You always were the clever ones. To the fellow survivors of "the" basement suite—solidarity, ladies. I thought of throwing in a few sewage backups, but I didn't think anyone would believe a place this gross would actually be rented to humans.

Thank you to my teenage consultants—Kiana, Morgan MacLeod and Oceanna Juhlke—for taking on some interesting questions without flinching! I appreciate your unique insights.

There are three people I will always be thankful for: Jocelyn Brown, Marina Endicott and Sarah Harvey. Jocelyn and Marina, you made me believe I could be a writer and took those first early steps with me. Sarah, you picked *Rodent* out of a slush pile and started me on the path I am now on. And your patience with my sentence fragments. Your medal is coming in the mail!

Thank you to the readers, friends, teachers and administrators who support my writing. It's an honor to be able to share my stories with you.

Thank you to friends (and friends of friends) on Facebook who respond to my random writing questions with enthusiasm. Thanks, Mike Fisher and Dean Walker, for answering my trucking and military questions. Any mistakes and omissions on those topics are my own.

Last but not least, thank you to my husband, Mike (also counselor extraordinaire), and my children, Liam, Maia (the queen of Would You Rather) and Anna. You are the spice of life and always patient with the long hours I spend writing and editing. (And I can't forget Chloe the cat, who's a great writing buddy and so worth the allergies.)

LISA J. LAWRENCE grew up as a free-range kid in small towns in British Columbia and Alberta, calling Stettler, Alberta, her hometown. She graduated from the University of Alberta with a BA in Romance Languages, an MA in Italian Studies and a BEd in Secondary Education. She currently works as a writer and Spanish teacher in Edmonton, Alberta, where she lives with her husband and three children.

Her first novel, *Rodent*, was nominated for a White Pine Award and a Snow Willow Award, longlisted for an Alberta Readers' Choice Award and was a finalist for the George Bugnet Award for Fiction. *Trail of Crumbs* is her second novel for young adults.

Find her on Facebook at Lisa J. Lawrence or follow @lawrenceauthor on Twitter.